The Book Hunter's Disciple

AIRSHIP 27 PRODUCTIONS

TM

The Book Hunter's Disciple
© 2024 Barbara Doran

Published by Airship 27 Productions
www.airship27.com
www.airship27hangar.com

Interior illustrations © 2024 Gary Kato
Cover illustration © 2024 Guy Davis

Editor: Ron Fortier
Associate Editor: Gordon Dymowski
Marketing and Promotions Manager: Michael Vance
Art Director/Designer: Rob Davis

ISBN: 978-1-953589-83-5

Printed in the United States of America

10 9 8 7 6 5 4 3 2 1

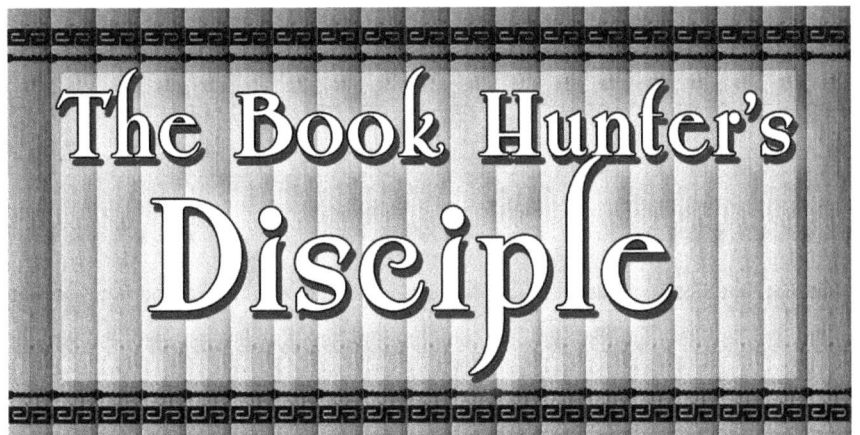

The Book Hunter's Disciple

by Barbara Doran

Chapter 1
Crows of Flame and Smoke

"It's getting away!"

"Don't stand there like an idiot. MOVE!!"

"AHHH!"

"Where is it?"

"Under the bed!"

"Quick, block it!"

"Ow! It bit me!"

"It's a scroll. How the hell can it bite you?"

"I don't know how. I just know it did!"

"Well, now you let it get away."

"It can't go far. It's just a scroll."

"It's already gone through half the mansion."

"Oh. Yeah."

Zhi Wenku watched the two boys struggle, stumbling over their own feet and each other's. She waved her fan slowly, trying not to laugh or mock. They were trying, bless their foolish little hearts. They were just failing far too often.

"For the Gods' sake, don't let it out of the room." A young man in the black and gold uniform of the Kirin Guard blocked the scroll's path to the door. Captain Li was calmer than his young companions and clearly the one in charge. "I don't want to chase it all the way around the building again."

Deciding enough was enough, Zhi Wenku glanced at her apprentice, who'd just finished sealing the windows with talismans. Good. The scroll shouldn't be going that way any time soon. It might have absorbed enough *qi* to be semi-sentient but it'd take more than that to break through.

"Done?" she asked. "Then take care of this thing before it breaks something valuable."

Qing didn't remind her it'd already taken out a half-dozen vases, a painting and a silk quilt. Instead he drew his newly acquired whisk from his sleeve, its dragon mane strands drifting on a non-existent breeze. The scroll dodged and dashed, slipping past the taller and lighter-haired of the two guards, slamming into Qing's chest as if it thought it could knock him over.

It couldn't. Qing had done some growing in the last year. His human form might appear slender and light, but he was a great deal too solid for a mere scroll to budge. It was the one thrown back, landing on the ground, pretending to be dead.

"Careful," Captain Li ordered. Not that the shorter of his companions paid him any mind. Impulsively, he threw himself at the thing, trying to tackle it, only to miss when the scroll jerked sideways and up, rushing for the nearest window.

The talismans flared. Burned. And to Zhi Wenku's great surprise, blew out. Was it a Great Work after all? But how in the name of the Gods could one of those have gotten so far from home? She'd have to investigate that as soon as this job was over. If it was a Great Work there was no telling what sort of trouble it might cause outside.

As the scroll tore through the window's paper and escaped, Zhi Wenku sighed, waving her fan at her apprentice. "Transform and catch it, boy." She could have chased it herself, but Qing needed the experience. "Be quick," she added as he obeyed, clothing dropping to the floor beneath him.

A moment later what had been an attractive—albeit wide-eyed and foolish looking—human in simple traveler's clothes became several times longer and covered in white, blue, purple and green scales. He'd been a Royal Blue Koi before he'd transcended to dragon carp, and now dragonling, stage.

Both boys shrieked, startled by Qing's sudden transformation. The silly fools had chased a living scroll through Count Li of Chang'an's mansion this whole afternoon and they couldn't handle a baby dragon? At least Captain Li— Count Li's nephew—remained calm, picking up Qing's clothes and handing them to Zhi Wenku without comment.

"Thank you, young man." Zhi Wenku shook her head at her apprentice's forgetfulness as Qing flowed through the window and flung himself into the air, flying after the scroll at top speed.

Once the pair faded from sight, she turned her attention on the other three. "The question is," she asked calmly, "Are you lot capable of keeping your mouths shut about this or do I have to put a spell of forgetfulness on you?" Because the last thing she and her apprentice needed was outsiders poking around in Book Hunter business.

弟子

The scroll was unexpectedly powerful, but it wasn't as fast or strong as Qing. No matter how high it flew over the landscape, it couldn't escape Qing's sight. He soared after it, riding thermals to loft himself higher.

As he rose, wind blowing through his mane, catching at his whiskers and barbels, he admired the view. Count Li Yongzhi's mansion was on

Hongqing Mountain, but a few miles east of Chang'an, surrounded by brilliant autumn foliage. From here, Qing saw the city, settled and secure, stone walls surrounding neatly laid out suburbs.

The moment of distraction gave the scroll a chance to slip further away, to Qing's self-annoyance. He knew what Master Zhi would say if she learned he'd been gawking instead of chasing. She'd be right. He'd a job to do. It was high time he did it.

Gathering his *qi*, he focused his attention on the scroll. It danced closer then flew backwards. He didn't know who'd created it but at a guess they'd like to tease. The only reason it'd bitten that one guard was because he'd grabbed too hard. Qing knew better.

The scroll had one advantage over Qing. Being small and light, it could shift position and direction a great deal faster than he could. It swirled near Qing, almost catching itself on his claw. "Now don't be stupid," he grumbled at it. "You'll get torn and then I'll be the one having to repair you."

It jumped around and he swore he heard it giggle. Books and scrolls generally didn't make noise, aside from rustling paper or clicking bamboo, but this one managed something. Was it his imagination? It was hard to tell with the wind blowing so strong in his flattened ears.

Again the scroll swung close. Again he missed catching it. He'd expected to, of course. This wouldn't be easy. At least the thing wasn't dangerous. Not like an Ancient Work who held the power to incinerate or disintegrate or melt you into goo. Those weren't playful, thank goodness. Or none of the ones who'd deigned to acknowledge him were.

He twisted and curled his body, pretending to be frustrated. "Come on, you rotten pest! Stop fiddling around! Let me catch you!"

The damned thing giggled again. Yes, this one's writer was definitely one of the more mischievous types. This wasn't the first of its kind he'd chased. It wouldn't be the last.

He gathered his *qi* for the next big effort. As the scroll sidled closer, tempting him to grab, tempting him to chase, he curled around, bringing his tail up behind it. Most dragons had too much dignity to use their hind ends like giant scoops. Most dragons hadn't started out as koi fish who'd spent their days doing acrobatic stunts for their royal master.

As his tail twisted into place, he spun sideways, slapping the strands of his mane around the scroll. It shrieked. Struggled. Fought. Almost broke free. But his hairs weren't just part of his body. They were the manifestation of his personal weapon, the Book Hunter's whisk, and they contained the same energy; an energy specially designed to calm overly excited books.

If the scroll had been a true Great Work it would've broken free. Qing was just an apprentice, not yet promoted to discipleship. He'd barely earned his whisk and the spells it contained were the weakest of their kind. Fortunately, though the scroll was strong, Qing was stronger.

As the thing calmed down, Qing gathered it close in his forelimbs and examined it for damage. "The Artifice of Design, by Dai Qingfu," he read aloud. "Master Zhi will appreciate meeting you. She's always looking for artifact lore."

It didn't respond, leaving Qing unsure if he'd actually heard it earlier. Whatever. He'd tell his Master and let her decide what to do. Speaking of which, it was high time he headed back to Li Mansion. He turned, intending to do so, only to stop and stare at what appeared to be a dark and smoky cloud, flying towards Chang'an from the southern mountain range. A storm? He'd feel a storm, surely.

The cloud seethed. Twisted. Shuddered. Screeched. Clouds didn't screech and though Qing knew not to get too close he wanted to know what the thing was. He flew towards it, meaning to stop long before he was in its path. Except part of it noticed his presence, shifting away from the main flock.

And flock it was. A gigantic flock of birds, or so they appeared at first. Now he recognized them from his texts. Not true crows, but manifestations of the Pot of Ten Thousand Crows, an ancient and deadly device that created birds of pure smoke and flame.

The fire crows cawed mockingly, too fast to easily escape. He wrapped his forelimbs tight around the scroll. Wrapped his *qi* around both it and himself. Flew off at top speed for the only safety he could find. He couldn't lead them back to Li Mansion or any inhabited area. Not without putting innocents at risk. All he could do was head for Wei River and hope the damned things lost his trail once he got there.

弟子

Persuading Captain Li Aiheng and his two charges to keep their silence took longer than Zhi Wenku liked. By this time they'd gone outside to keep an eye out for Qing. All while Kang Qiyun, the taller and rangier of the two boys, struggled to explain just how marvelous it would be for everyone to know a dragon, a real dragon, had descended to Earth.

The argument would have gone on longer but Zhi Wenku noticed a pillar of smoke rising west of them, half-hidden by the trees covering the slopes of the mountain. "What's that?" she demanded, though she'd a sneaking suspicion she already knew.

Li Aiqing, Captain Li's younger brother and the shorter of the two boys said, "Chang'an's on fire!"

"How do you know that?" Kang Qiyun demanded, thrusting gloved hands through his shaggy brown mane. He looked surprisingly distressed, as if Chang'an burning were a personal insult.

"It's obvious."

"How is it obvious? We can't see Chang'an from here."

"You never think."

"Oh, and you do?"

Captain Li snapped sharply, "Would the two of you please shut up?"

To Zhi Wenku's relief, the boys actually did, both hunching over in clear embarrassment. "Honestly," she grumbled. "I'd be done with this already if you'd stop arguing with each other."

Not bothering to wait for their apologies, she headed for a break in the trees. Li Aiqing was right. The smoke was from a fire and the fire was in Chang'an.

A chill went through her at the thought. The Soul Protection Society's headquarters were in Chang'an, and so was her dear friend Shen Wei. Was he there, working? Was he at risk? He was a powerful cultivator, she reminded herself. He and his fellow society members would be well enough. Xinglu, his apprentice, would surely keep him safe.

She hesitated. Book Hunters were equipped to deal with small fires, but this went beyond her skills; at least on her own. Qing could help, if he called in rain to douse the flames, but Qing was still chasing that silly scroll. At least she hoped he was chasing that silly scroll. He'd better not be fighting that fire by himself.

Turning to Captain Li, she ordered, "Tell your uncle's secretary I've gone to deal with a problem. I'll make sure the scroll is safe, so he shouldn't need to concern himself."

"Understood."

"But..." That last came from the boys, who apparently wanted to talk more.

"Don't argue with me. Just remember not to say a word about what Qing is. He's a baby, not an idol to be worshipped."

One calm agreement from Captain Li. Two nervous smiles from his companions. Zhi Wenku could only hope the captain could restrain those boys and keep them out of trouble. Gods knew why one of the An Emperor's elite had such a job, but it seemed to be his main purpose.

Drawing her flying whisk from her sleeve, Zhi Wenku enlarged it, setting it floating so she could rise above the trees. Chang'an was definitely on fire. Smoke towards the southwest, starting from a conflagration in the houses on the eastern edge of the city.

No. Wait. There was something wrong about that smoke. There were too many plumes; some blowing west across the city, a thicker and darker one streaming southeast. Yet again she corrected herself. That last plume didn't originate in the city. It flowed towards Chang'an, with a smaller plume sheering off north.

She adjusted her vision for great distance. Looked again.

Oh dear. Not smoke at all. A flock of fire crows setting the city alight. She turned her attention on the smaller group, watching them spiral around a spot near the Wei River. Rainclouds gathered overhead, thunder rumbling softly in the distance.

She knew what that meant. Her apprentice didn't seek trouble but he was a past master at finding it. Sighing, knowing just where the silly dragonling had gone, Zhi Wenku reached into her *qiankun* sleeve for her battle whisk. She'd no doubt her boy could douse those damned birds if he put his mind to it.

The question was, had he caught that scroll and did he remember to protect it?

弟子

Qing swam below the river's surface, watching the fire crows swirl overhead, clearly waiting for him to come out. "I can stay here all day," he snarled, though he doubted they could hear or would care if they did. He could stay there, yes, but that'd put anyone in the area in danger.

Thunder rolled in the distance, shuddering through him, making his heart pulse with every crash. It took him several seconds to realize why it felt so close and why it felt like it flowed through his veins. It was his. His storm, drawn to him by his fear and panic.

A faint flicker of natural *qi* answered his call, as if there were a spirit stone somewhere in the area. But, no. The sensation died almost as soon as he noticed it. Likely it was just the effect of his own *qi* on the surroundings. An echo of his growing power, coming back to him.

Qing wasn't supposed to bring down storms or rain. He was too young to control the power properly and storms and rain brought floods and other disasters with them. It was because he was scared and struggling to protect both himself and the scroll in his arms.

He had to calm himself. By now Master Zhi would have noticed both the fire crows and the storm. By now she'd be on her way to him, coming to help. He focused his thoughts, drawing on his core to settle his power and make the storm go away.

Except a scream, barely audible this deep in the water, drew his attention.

Not good. He'd drifted along with the current towards a small group of fishing boats. If he were alone, he could stay put. But those fire crows would target the fishermen.

He let the storm grow, flinging himself out of the water into lightning embroidered clouds, protecting the shivering scroll in his forelimbs. Loosing the rain set the crows screaming, flying back the way they'd come. As the boats scudded across wind driven river waters, he hoped his storm wouldn't put the men in danger.

"Stay focused!"

That was Master Zhi, showing up just in time. Desperately grateful, he called out, "They're getting away! Can you help?"

"Already on it," Master Zhi called back, spinning her battle whisk in an intricate pattern. Her sorcery was always so elegant and quiet compared to his. It was also several times more effective. The storm winds spun round them, holding the fire crows in place while Qing's rain doused them thoroughly.

It only took a minute for the hundred or so crows to turn to sodden ash, falling into the river below. Master Zhi turned her attention on Chang'an. "Let's put the rest of that rain to good use."

"Yes, ma'am." They flew towards the fire, spotting members of the Soul Protection Society dousing flames as commoners ran screaming for cover. Small blame to them. They'd little to save them except their fast moving feet.

The storm followed Qing, rain sizzling through both fire crows and their flames. Feeling his lightning trying to strike, Qing forced himself under control. They didn't need a bolt hitting something or someone down there.

At last the fire crows were gone and their fires with them. Qing could tell they'd come too late to save some houses. Too late to save some people. He tried not to think about it as he and Master Zhi landed in the courtyard of the Soul Protection Society.

Several guards rushed towards them, weapons readied. They'd never visited the Society's Headquarters before, so it was no surprise they weren't recognized as Master Shen Wei's friends. Still, Qing wasn't in a good mood about the whole thing. "Do we have to?"

"We should make sure they know who we are. No point in making them think we were behind those damned crows," Master Zhi told him. "Do you have the scroll?"

Trust Master Zhi to have her priorities straight. Qing handed the trembling thing over. "Should I change?"

She stroked the scroll, quieting it, then put it in her sleeve for later. "You left your clothes behind, silly dragonling. We'll wait until we're private."

Before Qing could apologize, the guards were there, surrounding them with magic engraved spears. Their eyes were wide and scared, yet they were prepared to fight, despite him being several times their size.

"Fetch Master Alchemist Shen if you would," Master Zhi told the obvious leader. "I'm his friend, Master Zhi Wenku of the Book Hunters. We need to talk." She paused. Glanced at Qing. "Though first we need a private room so my apprentice can change."

CHAPTER 2
Death on the Mountain

Shen Wei's arrival was accompanied by an argument. Several men and women spoke over each other and Shen Wei too. Most of the speakers' voices were too muffled to make out. One, by virtue of his greater lung capacity and obvious irritation, was clearer.

"Just because I'm half fire demon does not mean I'm behind every damned fire in the area. How many times do I have to say that?"

Qing looked up from where he rested; dark eyes wide, black hair a tangled mess, pale skin smudged with smoke, smelling of river water. They'd been allowed a room and locked inside, but they'd been given nothing to let him clean himself. In Zhi Wenku's opinion he needed a proper bath. How could he have made such a mess of himself that it'd transferred from his dragon to human form, anyway?

"I think Xinglu's ready to bite someone," Qing murmured.

"Xinglu best not if he wants to stay with Shen Wei," Zhi Wenku retorted. Xinglu's father had been a houdou, a hell-born hound with an affinity for flames. It wasn't surprising some folk thought he'd had something to do with the fire. Foolish, but not surprising.

The door rattled open and Shen Wei entered with a disgusted air. "Honestly," he snapped at someone behind him. "You've no evidence they were even involved in the fire. What business did you have treating them like a pair of criminals?" At the same time his fan showed the words, [[Deepest apologies, my dear.]]

Zhi Wenku couldn't help smiling, using her fan to answer with, [[It's not your fault to apologize for.]] Really, she'd expected this. Shen Wei might be head of the Soul Protection Society's Alchemist Division but that didn't mean his fellow cultivationists would respect her just because she'd used his name.

Xinglu pushed in behind his master and Zhi Wenku raised a brow at the big lad. He'd grown in the month or so since she'd seen him last. His broad features and coarse black hair remained unchanged, but he towered over everyone else. Smoke trailed from his nostrils, sure sign he was at the end of his temper.

Automatically, because Shen Wei would suffer if Xinglu got in trouble, Zhi Wenku stood and swatted him lightly atop his head with her fan. "Mind your manners this instant."

As was often the case, Xinglu winced and flushed. "Yes, Auntie."

"And don't call me Auntie."

"No, Auntie."

She rolled her eyes. Turned from him. Looked at the men and women demanding Shen Wei's attention. "I realize I'm an outsider with no business telling you your business, but that fire was set by fire crows, as you ought to have noticed. In all likelihood they came from the Pot of Ten Thousand Crows. Not a half-houdou child."

They stared at her and one, a querulous older man in dark brown, snapped, "That's locked away in the Emperor's treasury! There's no way it could have something to do with this!"

Now that was interesting. Zhi Wenku hadn't realized that particular artifact was—or had been—in the hands of An Kingdom's Emperor. "Then someone's either found a way to imitate the pot's powers or managed to steal it."

The man tightened his lips. "Or you could be a liar protecting your lover's so-called disciple."

Before Qing or Xinglu or even Zhi Wenku could react, Shen Wei's fan blocked her accuser's way. "Senior Yao," he murmured softly. "Master Zhi Wenku is an honored senior member of the Book Hunters. The Book Hunters are, if not allies, respected colleagues. Accusing her of lying for any reason is an insult. One I trust you have the spiritual fortitude to back up?"

That silenced Senior Yao. Then, "This one apologizes," he muttered, not sorry at all. "This cultivator spoke out of turn."

"We'll discuss this further, later," Shen Wei said, turning to face the others. "As I said, Xinglu was with me at the auction house on the other side of the city. There's no reason to blame him for the fire and plenty to thank him for helping save people. Nor does his ancestry make him responsible every time there's a fire."

"But...."

"No buts. If my fellow division heads, or Chief Cultivator Li, ask for details, I will tell them. But you lot are in no position to speak against either of us. Now run along, children. Master Zhi and I have important business to discuss."

It took several minutes of arguing, and one sharp bark from Xinglu, to send the other cultivators scurrying off. Then, with a weary sigh, Shen Wei turned back to Zhi Wenku. "Now then, my dear. You said it was the Pot of Ten Thousand Crows? I don't suppose you know anything more?" At the same time dozens of flowers—roses, mostly—appeared on the surface of his fan.

"I have an idea of where it was used," Zhi Wenku told him, touching her fan to his lightly to accept the small gift, returning it with a portrait of a bamboo garden. "Shall we go?"

"Of course, my dear. I don't know if those crows came from that pot, or if someone found a way to imitate it, but we'd best find out and quickly."

Zhi Wenku didn't know either and wasn't sure which would be worse.

弟子

Qing, having spotted the fire crows first, knew best which way to head. He couldn't be sure exactly where they'd started from, but he could guide them to the right area.

Master Shen and Xinglu flew on their swords, Master Zhi on her whisk. And, of course, Qing just took dragonling form again, remembering to transform all his clothing this time. Embarrassing to realize he'd left them behind for his master to pick up. She wasn't going to let him live that one down any time soon.

"Your rain came timely," Master Shen told him as they flew. "Xinglu was eating as much of the fire as he could, but we couldn't keep up."

Qing couldn't smile without looking hungry, but he was pleased. "I only started the storm because I was scared. They were hunting me, too."

"As ill-luck would have it, he drew their attention while chasing a scroll," Master Zhi added by way of explanation, patting her Warehouse where it resided in her sleeve. "Speaking of which.... is your Chief Cultivator Li related to Count Li Yongzhi?"

"He is the Count. How does he come into the matter?"

Master Zhi frowned. "His secretary called me in to chase down that scroll I mentioned. An odd coincidence, and you know how I feel about those."

Master Shen chuckled. "I do. I'd also note that coincidences do happen and that Master Li has a way of becoming involved in dangerous situations." He fanned himself gently, the silk and paper surface forming the words, [[Like most of us, really.]]

Puzzled, Qing asked, "If Count Li is Chief Cultivator of the Soul Protection Society, why wouldn't he know he had a Great Work? Or at least a sentient one?"

"A Great Work?"

Realizing he'd used a Book Hunter term, Qing explained, "A Great Work is a writing by a powerful cultivator or sorcerer who's imbued it with some of their power. There are lesser works that gain self-awareness, but this one was awfully strong."

"I'd think such books would be carefully protected," Master Shen murmured. "And you've never mentioned anything of the sort before."

"They aren't common outside of Khaitan, given how much magic they need to transcend." A wave of Master Zhi's fan was accompanied by the words, [[We've had other, more interesting things to discuss.]]

As Master Shen blushed, Qing glanced at Xinglu and they both rolled their eyes. Really, these two still acted like giddy teenagers when it came to their painfully slow courtship. By now a fish or a dragon or a demon would have found time to get properly acquainted so they wouldn't spend all their spare moments flirting.

Returning to the subject, Master Shen told Qing, "If it was at the Count's mansion then he may not have known about it yet. He doesn't spend much time there at all. He prefers his tower at the Society."

Ah. That didn't make complete sense but Qing didn't pretend to understand humans. He was about to say as much when he noticed how close they were to their destination. "I think those fire crows started from somewhere around here."

"They did," Xinglu said suddenly. "I can smell traces of their passage."

Qing let Xinglu take the lead. They swung around, circling over the trees covering the hillside, while Xinglu sniffed the air. Then he paled. "Master... there's burned meat."

They followed him towards a small clearing, where a half-dozen partially charred figures smoldered, their lower halves whole and unburned. Qing's storm hadn't helped them. Qing's storm couldn't have helped them. It was obvious whatever hit them had hit fast; too fast to even realize they were killed.

The bodies knelt around the center of the clearing, in a circle of unburned grass, its center flattened. From their positions, they'd been focused on whatever had been there when they'd died. Two had their hands stretched out, clutching at something.

"Poor fools," Master Shen murmured. "I don't know if the thing they had was the real Pot of Ten Thousand Crows or an imitation, but it's obvious they'd no clue what they were opening. Thank the Gods it didn't set the forest alight in the process. Autumn is the worst time for a fire."

"Indeed," Master Zhi murmured, gazing at the scene thoughtfully. "Though some questions occur to me. First, why did the crows head straight for Chang'an? There's at least one or two small villages between here and their target."

"A good question. Unfortunately, one I have no answer to." Master Shen eyed the bodies thoughtfully and added, "I believe I know your second question. Namely, where exactly is the thing they opened?"

Qing blinked. He been too busy reacting to these poor people's deaths to consider that. "You mean?"

"I mean opening that damned pot wouldn't destroy it. Even if it did, there'd be some signs. Their lower bodies are uninjured, suggesting the fire that consumed them was blocked by whatever contained it. That means there was something here when they died. Something not here now."

"We have to find it," Master Zhi said quietly, not even pretending she'd stay out of this matter. "Find it and whomever took it. Before they start a fire Qing's rain can't stop."

弟子

Shen Wei sent a brass messenger bird back to his Society, telling them he needed someone to collect the bodies while they explored the area searching for clues. Not that they found much of anything. Zhi Wenku was almost certain the victims hadn't intended to release fire crows on Chang'an. They surely hadn't intended to die doing so.

"I am an alchemist, not a historian," Shen Wei said as they searched around. "I know the founder of the previous dynasty—Kang Huang—owned the Pot of Ten Thousand Crows. What I don't know is exactly what it was."

"It's mentioned in Ho Wen's Compendium of Artifacts and Devices," Zhi Wenku told him, visualizing and quoting the relevant passage. "Created by an unknown craft-master of great skill and even greater cruelty, the pot contains the essence of sun crows tortured by darkness. When it's opened in full daylight, it releases resentful *qi* that take the form of fire crows. It, along with a bow called Ten Thousand Miles of Smoke, once destroyed the city of Jianxian."

Xinglu looked up. "Is Jianxian in Khaitan, Auntie? I've never heard of it."

She ignored the honorific, knowing he wouldn't let go of it now. "You haven't heard of it because there's nothing left of the place. I'd have to consult a map, but I believe the region is called Yulin now." Zhi Wenku's memory was best when it came to words. Images required reminders.

The information clearly didn't make Shen Wei happy. His fan went blank, sign he was too deep in thought to offer commentary. He turned his gaze from the location of the pot to the direction its contents had flown.

"Master Shen?" Qing asked, "Is something wrong?"

"Someone controlled the fire crows once they were released." When they all looked at him, wondering how he could tell, he pointed at the trees. "The branches are charred in a distinctive and even pattern. The things held position for a brief period of time. The char doesn't go deep. It also doesn't touch the upper side of the trees."

Visualizing the situation, Zhi Wenku gestured as if she were stroking the sides of a sphere, bringing her hands up along a pipe at the top. "They rose high enough to find Chang'an, then headed straight for it."

"And chased me because I saw where they came from?" Qing wondered.

Possibly. "You're a very young dragonling but you're strong enough to summon enough rain to put the fire out. Whomever controlled the fire crows would have known you were a risk to their plans."

Xinglu protested, "But who'd want to burn Chang'an? I mean, I can see invading. The Emperor's barely adult and no one's sure what to make of him. But burn it to the ground? Overkill."

It absolutely was and Zhi Wenku was about to say so when she heard people moving through the nearby woods. Instinctively, she fell silent, using her fan to ask Shen Wei, [[Your people?]]

[[They'd fly in,]] he told her, looking mildly concerned.

They gathered together, weapons close to hand, as a troop of soldiers dressed in similar uniforms as Captain Li's stalked into the clearing. Their leader was a middle-aged man with a great deal more brocade on his surcoat. Clearly someone of importance.

Whomever he was, he took his work more seriously than those three back at the mansion. He glared at the sight of them, hand on his weapon as he stepped forward. "You are?"

Shen Wei cupped his hands. Bowed politely, calling the leader by name. "Greet you, Commander Fan. This Shen Wei is a member of the Soul Protection Society," he explained. "We came to investigate the source of the recent fire."

The commander frowned, brows drawn together tightly. "Fire?"

"Yes, sir. Just an hour or so ago. You must have been out of the city when it happens." As Commander Fan opened his mouth, clearly meaning to ask more, Shen Wei raised a hand. "Before you ask why we're investigating so far from the city, I point out our not particularly lively companions."

The gesture towards the bodies behind them made Commander Fan look, frowning furiously. "The hell? They're from the Black Boulder Gang. We were just out here looking for them!"

That was exactly when several dozen poorly dressed men, faces covered in heavy black cloth, arrived on the other side of the clearing. "Funny that," a dark-clad man carrying an iron umbrella said loudly. "We were jus' lookin' for 'em too, Commander Fan."

弟子

The newcomer felt strange. Looked strange, for that matter. Tall, dressed in poorly repaired black robes, his shaggy dark hair hung around a face that belonged on a southern idol, or would have if it weren't smudged with dirt. He looked a beggar and felt like a king of hell. Pale eyes scanned the clearing; sharp and dangerous and cold.

Qing stayed quiet, knowing better than to draw attention. Xinglu wasn't quite so calm, his instinctive sense of threat making him glower at the newcomer, lips curled back from his teeth, a soft growl humming in his throat. If Master Shen weren't blocking him with his fan, Qing was sure his best friend would be rushing to the attack already.

Fortunately for all concerned, Xinglu held his ground. One of Commander Fan's men, on the other hand, didn't. "PANG HUA!" he shouted, starting forward angrily. "YOU DOG! I'LL TAKE YOU IN!"

The bandit leader tilted his head, revealing an intricate black and silver tattoo at the base of his throat. He eyed the Commander with an amused air, playing with his weapon in a negligent fashion. Qing couldn't help wonder at the thing; who carried an umbrella into a fight, even if it was iron and had a needle sharp ferrule?

Commander Fan snagged his man before he got more than three steps. "Shut up!" he growled. "Did you hear me order an attack?" His fingers flickered behind him as he spoke, just visible from Qing's position. Whatever the motion meant, it quieted the other guards. The four furthest back silently faded into the woods.

The bandits had all their attention on the argument in front of them. Commander Fan seemed to have his work cut out for him, getting his man under control, and the bandits were clearly amused. Pang Hua chuckled, "I'm loving a good fight, but all this fussing's gonna get someone killed. Y'know how I'm feeling 'bout wasteful killing."

A scoff from Commander Fan. "If you're suggesting you're against it, try some other lie. That one's covered in mold." As Pang Hua laughed, the Commander continued, "You don't usually waste time with talk. What are you lot up to?"

"I meant t'fetch them idiots o'er there afore they got their fool selves in trouble. Too late." Pang Hua waved a negligent hand towards the bodies at the center of the clearing, then at a skinny kid who clearly hadn't eaten much in this life and possibly not his previous either. "They're not supposed t'take jobs on their own but Little Worm here come told me they got hired to pick something up and bring it out here. Looks t'me like they got what they came for."

That was a horribly callous reaction to one's people dying, Qing thought.

He wondered how long the man had been there, watching and listening to Masters Shen and Zhi discuss the artifact. The man showed signs of being reasonably intelligent, despite his speech and his manner. Whatever he knew, he kept close to his chest.

Commander Fan looked towards the victims. "Then they are your people. I thought I recognized Number Three Baldy's club foot."

Was that how he knew who the dead men were? Qing didn't dare ask. Didn't dare interrupt. Not that it mattered, because that was when the few men Commander Fan had ordered off earlier came around behind Pang Hua's men and set to attack.

It was also the moment a dozen Society cultivators, led by that irritating Senior Yao, arrived to collect the bodies.

Chapter 3
Unexpected Alliances

Zhi Wenku drew Qing out of the way. That wasn't their business. A Kingdom's Kirin Guard were elite of the elite. They could handle a band of poorly trained, poorly fed, bandits. As for Senior Yao and his fellow cultivationists, they'd their own work to do.

Noting Xinglu tilting his head, watching the fight hungrily, Zhi Wenku snatched hold of his ear and dragged him back as well. "Stay out unless your master says you can," she ordered. Shen Wei was busy with Senior Yao and had no time to spare for his impetuous apprentice.

Some apprentices would have complained that she wasn't the boss of them. Xinglu knew better. "Yes, Auntie," he muttered, still watching the fight. At least now his expression was just wistful. Hopefully that meant he really would listen and behave.

Behind them, Senior Yao complained, "Why did you bring us to a fight? We're not swordsmen."

"You have swords," Shen Wei pointed out. "And if you practiced the way our Chief Cultivator expects us all to, you'd be in no danger."

A bandit crashed into Senior Yao, knocking him over only because Shen Wei stepped out of the man's path as he was flung across the clearing. That left both men sprawled atop one of the bodies, both exclaiming with furious disgust.

"Shen Wei, you BASTARD!" Senior Yao shouted, struggling to rise.

"Yes. Yes, I am." Shen Wei turned his attention back to the fight, gesturing at his fellow cultivators to do their job. "I'll keep them away from you while

"THEN THEY ARE YOUR PEOPLE."

you work. Xinglu, keep an eye on the main pair. My dear, would you and Qing be willing to help?"

"All you had to do was ask," Zhi Wenku told him, gesturing at Qing to take a position that put him—sort of—towards the back of the fight. "Don't do anything too obvious, please."

Given Qing's markings had darkened with excitement, it was a necessary warning. The boy didn't like fighting much, but he was a dragonling and they didn't do fear the way humans did. He might transform out of sheer enthusiasm.

The four of them watched the fight, pointedly staying out of it as it surged back and forth around the edges of the clearing. The Kirin Guards were—as expected—an excellent team. They took turns dodging between the less skilled bandits, knocking them down and out with ease. Really, if it weren't for Pang Hua, the fight would have been over within minutes and not in the bandits' favor.

That strange weapon of Pang Hua's made him even more formidable. Zhi Wenku suspected he'd be Commander Fan's match with a normal sword or saber. The umbrella turned their fight from mere skill to a combination of finesse and expertise. It also made it something of a farce.

Both men moved almost blindingly fast, even to Zhi Wenku's sharp eyes. Pang Hua thrust the pointed tip of his weapon at the Commander, only to have Commander Fan arch backwards, sliding towards his enemy with his sword cutting across Pang Hua's chest. Or, rather, where Pang Hua's chest had been. By the time Commander Fan reached him, he'd twisted out of the way.

Another movement and it was Commander Fan's turn to thrust and his turn to miss. Not because Pang Hua dodged, either. The umbrella opened, an iridescent pattern shimmering on its surface, its design similar to the tattoo on the man's throat. Spinning, it caught the blade and sent it off at an angle. Suddenly it switched directions, sharpened struts catching hold of Commander Fan's wrist, twisting it around. He barely kept his blade in hand, using an offhand dagger to strike back.

That blow was kicked away almost mockingly, though Pang Hua didn't say a word as he fought. Commander Fan's lips tightened and he spun around, trying to strike again, only to have his hand engulfed when the umbrella inverted around it. He struggled to break free, to twist his sword against the silk of the umbrella, but could only stumble and flail helplessly, trapped.

Quite suddenly Pang Hua glanced towards the center of the clearing. Laughed. "Well, that's enough of that," he said. "Looks like neither of us get what we want." He swung his weapon, lifting Commander Fan off his feet. At the end of the arc, the umbrella refolded itself properly, releasing Commander Fan's hand.

As the Captain flew through the air into the forest, Pang Hua flung a handful of something dark and odorous into the air, creating a dense cloud of stench and shadow.

When it was gone, so were he and all his men.

弟子

It took some discussion between Commander Fan and Master Shen to get him to agree to the Soul Protection Society taking the bodies. If they were right and the Pot of Ten Thousand Crows was involved, that made it Society business, much to Commander Fan's obvious irritation.

Qing waited until they were on their way back to Chang'an and Soul Protection Society's headquarters before asking, "Why was Commander Fan so mad at you, Master Shen?"

Master Shen's fan asked, [[Not Unka Shen?]], but he didn't tease beyond that, saying, "The Kirin Guard has something of a distaste for the Society. Understandably so, given we're independenct from any government, but have so much power."

Xinglu added, "They're worried we might try to overthrow the Emperor, and he's their Lord and Commander."

The Book Hunters had a similar tradition and didn't have a problem in Khaitan. When Qing said so, however, Master Zhi corrected him. "The Book Hunters obey the rule of law in Khaitan. That means we have no more and no less position and responsibility than any other citizen."

"Whereas the Soul Protection Society holds more power, simply by virtue of being part of an existence most people in our lands have little contact with." Master Shen glanced behind them, to where Senior Yao and his companions were trailing behind, complaining over maintaining the array containing the bodies. "Some cultivators feel power alone gives us special rights. Don't scoff, Xinglu. Commander Fan is right to worry. Chief Cultivator Li defeated Emperor Kang Huang a century and a half ago."

Recalling what he knew about local politics and history, Qing thought he understood. The Kingdom's current Emperor—An Ranshi—wasn't a full adult yet. As the youngest and only survivor of his family's fight for the throne, he couldn't afford any threats to his power.

By now they'd reached Soul Protection Society's headquarters, giving Qing a chance to take a proper look at the place. He and Master Zhi had been in too much of a rush earlier for him to gawk like a village bumpkin first visiting a city.

The Society's headquarters were in the northwest corner of Chang'an, just a bit west of the Imperial City. Its pale walls were lower by a few feet, but half again as thick. Inside were a half-dozen buildings, laid out in a chaotic pattern suggesting its designers hadn't access to a square or any sort of straightedge.

Noticing one building off on its own, its outer walls heavily buttressed, Qing asked, "Is that where you develop weapons?" He pointed with his tail, a habit that he'd yet to break despite it being a faux-pas amongst true dragons.

Xinglu laughed. "In a way. That's the alchemical branch quarters. You know how often we blow up our pots. Our walls have to be tougher."

One of the group behind them grumbled, "And yet still you manage to get materials everywhere."

"And I don't even want to discuss the cost of keeping you lot in alchemy pots."

Qing had a strange vision of Xinglu and Master Shen actually in their alchemy pots, but understood the complaint even so. He'd watched his friend completely ruin three heavy stone pots in a row trying to concoct a Fifth Art pill for his master.

Coughing embarrassedly, Master Shen pointed to the courtyard beside the alchemy building. "We'll set down there. We'll have to examine the victims and I'd rather not drag them inside anywhere. Such a mess."

They landed, Qing returning to his human form so as to stay out of the way. At the same time, the seniors set their burdens down, then scattered to avoid being involved in the matter any longer, too disgusted by the stink of charred flesh to want to stay. Or, rather, they started to scatter, only to come to a dead halt when a soft voice said, "Wait."

Turning towards the sound, Qing saw a man standing beneath a scholar tree. He blinked in momentary confusion as something flashed across his eyes. It felt familiar but the memory shifted from his thoughts before he could focus on it.

The man stepped out of the shadows, slender shape half-concealed beneath robes of peacock greens and blues. Although his waist-length hair was alabaster white, his thin features appeared quite young and soft, with the distant air of a deity's statue. He held a delicate looking parasol, its pale surface marked with an intricate pattern in dark purple-tinted ink.

Immediately the Soul Protection Society members cupped their hands and bowed deeply, even Master Shen and Xinglu. Realizing Master Zhi was doing the same, Qing quickly followed suit. He didn't know this strange man but his cultivation was clearly far beyond those present. If he wasn't Count Li, the Chief Cultivator of the Soul Protection Society, he was still someone incredibly important.

Master Shen confirmed Qing's guess. "Greet you, Chief Cultivator. Apologies if our investigation has disturbed your meditations."

The faintest smile curved Count Li's lips and black eyes gleamed with humor. He spoke in a soft voice, "Please rise." As they all straightened he indicated Qing and his master. "These two are...."

Master Shen bowed again, murmuring. "This lady is Master Zhi Wenku, a member of the Book Hunter's Society. The young man is Qing, her apprentice."

"A dragonling is only an apprentice? Not yet a disciple?" Count Li asked, inclining his head at the two of them.

"He's barely fifty, Count Li," Master Zhi explained. "He keeps jumping up over obstacles and forgetting he's still a baby."

Some might have been embarrassed, but Qing knew she was right. From his first transcendence—pond koi to dragon-carp—to his current one, he'd gained power far too fast. He needed to take some time and build his foundations properly if he wanted to survive.

Count Li turned his attention on the dead. "And these?"

"From what I understand, they were members of the Black Boulder Gang. According to Commander Fan of the Kirin Guards, they'd robbed the Imperial Mausoleum last night. He doesn't know what they stole, but I believe they happened on a forgotten cache containing the artifact that caused that fire."

"The Pot of Ten Thousand Crows, correct?"

"Yes, Chief Cultivator. We believe it may have been. Or, if not, a horrifyingly accurate counterfeit."

"I'd hoped we were done with Kang Huang's artifacts," Count Li said cryptically as he walked slowly around the circle of dead men. "Master Zhi, would you know how long we have before it can be used again?"

A short thoughtful blink. "If it's the original, it takes a full month to recharge. I've no idea how long it'd take if it were a copy."

"Hmm." Count Li waved at the bodies. "You were right to bring them and the ground beneath them here as intact as possible. I'll have Master Tang scry what's left of them. I imagine you'd like to examine them afterwards?"

"I would, sir." Master Shen glanced at the remains, adding, "They're not intact, but what's left should be respected. If you'd have someone contact their families afterwards?"

"If they were from a gang, they likely didn't have many kin."

A slight bow. "True, sir. But criminals or not, those they left behind have a right to know their fate."

Count Li agreed and returned to Master Zhi. "The Book Hunters seldom involve themselves with any business but their own. Is it because you and my Shen Wei court that you're willing to take a hand in this matter?"

Some people might have evaded the question, but not Master Zhi. She quirked a smile. "I'm a busybody," she admitted. "I involved myself in the business with Zhu Kan last year without needing courtship to draw me in."

Count Li wasted no time on platitudes, saying, "Then I will gladly accept you and your apprentice's help. If you'd come with my Shen Wei when he reports, I'd appreciate it greatly."

Without waiting for confirmation, Count Li floated into the air, parasol carrying him towards the tallest tower at the center of the compound. When he was out of earshot, Shen Wei chuckled. "He likes to make an exit, I fear."

"Indeed," Master Zhi agreed. "Shall we get to work? It's getting late and I don't want to be at this all night."

Yawning wide and setting Xinglu yawning in response, Qing had to agree. He'd had a busy day and even strong young dragonlings like himself needed sleep.

弟子

The investigation of the bodies took a great deal longer than Zhi Wenku liked. In the end she'd had to make both Qing and Xinglu lie down off to the side. The boys were smart and often useful, but they'd spent much of their day dealing with dangerous situations. They needed rest.

The first step was the most difficult. Master Tang, a seemingly middle-aged cultivator who could have been anything from fifty to a hundred, examined the array the seniors had put around the bodies, scoffed, and set to creating a spell that would show brief images of what'd happened to its contents.

"Not my best work," Master Tang muttered when she was done.

The images were blurred and unfocused, showing only bits and pieces of the incident. Not enough to show exactly what happened but enough to confirm one thing. "We can see the base of whatever the dead men opened where it touched the ground," Zhi Wenku said. "It does appear to be the Pot of Ten Thousand Crows. The writing around the edge is as described in my Compendium of Artifacts and Devices."

Shen Wei's fan flickered with images of fire and devastation as his expression turned dark. "In which case, we need to find out how it was stolen and who was behind the theft."

"Surely it was that Black Boulder gang," Master Tang asked, removing her spell so the bodies could be lain out for examination.

"What your spell can't show is who took the pot after it was used," Shen Wei answered. "Not to mention those fire crows were being directed."

That had to be the case. The things didn't even have animal intelligence. Just a need to destroy whatever lay in their path. Lacking guidance, the fire crows would have burned the forest down, not headed straight for Chang'an. "The way some went after Qing suggests you're right." Zhi Wenku indicated the sprawled figure slumped against Xinglu, both boys snoring loudly.

"He's the dragonling I heard mentioned? I can see why the culprit would want him out of the way. His rain came well-timed."

By now Senior Yao and the others had put the bodies in what little order was possible, allowing Shen Wei to begin his task. They roused their sleepy apprentices, setting them to work taking notes, while they examined the victims' remains.

"Based on their upper halves being charred but not burned away entirely, the pot wasn't damaged," Shen Wei muttered.

"The lid had to have blown straight upwards," Zhi Wenku added. "The ones who had their hands on it lost their fingers. That and the burn damage is too even. It would have hit one side of the group harder if the lid blocked it."

"Interesting that the bodies didn't fall over," Shen Wei added. "Any thoughts on how that happened?"

"None," Zhi Wenku admitted.

They continued, finding little but a few small possessions. A pouch full of counterfeit coins. A partially charred braid embedded in one wrist. A doll, wrapped carefully and hidden in a tunic pocket, barely low enough to avoid being burnt away. The last made up Zhi Wenku's mind. Bandit though the victim was, they'd had someone they cared about. Someone would have to face justice for this.

At last they'd found all they could and it wasn't nearly enough. "Send the boys to bed and we'll report to Count Li."

Both Xinglu and Qing objected immediately. "We're not that sleepy." "We had a nap. You're the ones who haven't slept."

Shen Wei and Zhi Wenku were highly cultivated masters. They wouldn't need sleep for weeks. Still, it was obvious the boys wouldn't give up without a fight. "Fine. Come along, then," they said together, eliciting near identical smiles from the children.

They headed to the Chief Cultivator's tower and soon found themselves ushered into an elegant study lit by dozens upon dozens of night-luminescent pearls.

The furnishings were simple in a way that spoke of money and power: mahogany shelves, a low desk of lacquered wood and inset mother-of-pearl, ermine-hair brushes and a carved inkstone of white jade with a small figure of a boy carrying an umbrella, leaning over the inkwell to gaze at his reflection.

What drew Zhi Wenku's attention, however, was the bookshelves behind the desk. She'd have to take their contents out to be sure, but based on their titles, written in an elegant hand on their spines, Count Li's collection back at his mansion paled beside what he kept here.

She wondered if he'd let her examine it.

弟子

Qing mostly controlled his urge to gawk. He might be an inexperienced child but he didn't want a Near Immortal like Count Li to see how naïve he actually was. The fact that the man wasn't in the room didn't matter. He'd a feeling the Chief Cultivator would notice even if he wasn't there.

"This servant will inform the master that you await them," their guide said quietly, bowing as she exited.

"Of course." Master Shen seemed unconcerned by the Count's absence. Once the servant left, he continued, "Count Li spends most of his days in seclusion. Any time you want to speak to him you have to expect a wait."

"This isn't his office, then?" Master Zhi asked curiously. Typical of her, she moved closer to the books, apparently deciding it wouldn't be rude to take a look given this was a waiting room. She was probably right.

"No. No one's allowed in his actual rooms. He just uses this for meetings." Master Shen paused, clearly aware of how odd that sounded. "He's very private. His right, of course, given he founded the Society."

Qing couldn't help asking curiously, "When was that?" The Count looked in his twenties but Near Immortals could be thousands of years old and never show it.

After thinking about it a moment, Shen Wei told Qing, "Around a hundred and fifty years ago. Right at the end of Kang Huang's reign."

Kang Huang was the first emperor of the preceding dynasty. All Qing knew about him was that he was a cultivator as well, with a particular talent for creating artifacts. His oldest son had succeeded him, but was betrayed by his sister, Daoping. The girl had taken the throne after a bitter battle with her siblings, only to fall in turn to her own hubris. There wasn't much else in the history about her, no doubt because the dynasty had collapsed a decade or so later.

"You'll have to spend more time reading local history," Master Zhi suggested. "But not right now."

Since reading local history would require him going into the Warehouse and missing the discussion with Count Li, Qing agreed. Having little else to do but wait, Qing went to the window to gaze out at the Imperial City. It was quite late now and completely dark aside from the stars and torchlight, but he could dimly see the shapes of the neatly arranged buildings that made up the Emperor's home. Guards moved around the streets of the walled-in region, while others stood straight and attentive at their posts along that wall.

It surprised him that the Emperor didn't mind the Soul Protection Society having a tower tall enough to see into his courtyards. Was it because he trusted them? Or was he too afraid of their power to argue the point? Given what he'd been told so far, Qing suspected the latter.

A flicker of shadow drew Qing's attention. Something moved along the rooftops, evading the guards with practiced ease. An assassin? A thief? Something about their movements seemed familiar, rather like that bandit chief they'd met earlier that day. They carried an umbrella, just like Pang Hua had, flipping from one rooftop to another; light as a bit of thistledown on the wind, quick as a dragonfly in flight.

Qing was about to call his master's attention when that shadow paused, looked up at Qing, and raised a finger to masked lips. A voice spoke in Qing's thoughts. *Hush, little dragonling. Don't fuss.* The words were accompanied by an intricate gesture, one that flickered with a faint edge of *qi*.

Before Qing could react, that *qi* crossed the distance between the stranger and himself. There was a sharp twinge in Qing's throat and though he struggled to open his mouth and speak, he could not. Fear shuddered through him, strong enough that Xinglu sniffed the air and turned to look. "Qing? You all right?"

"I... can't tell." Even that was almost too much for him to manage. Whatever the shadowy figure had done, it was incredibly powerful. Panicked, he gestured sharply at his friend, drawing Xinglu over, hoping he'd see what Qing had. Except by now the stranger was gone.

"What is it?" Master Zhi asked, joining the two of them. "Something's wrong." She wasn't asking. Thank the Gods she wasn't asking. She understood enough to know Qing couldn't answer. Her fan fluttered between them with the words, [[You've been bespelled?]]

He couldn't speak but the geas on him wasn't complicated enough to prevent gestures. He touched his throat to confirm her suspicion. Again the fan fluttered, now with the words, [[Speech block? You saw something you shouldn't?]]

Again Qing agreed. "The Imperial City looks beautiful tonight. So safe and secure."

Now Master Shen used his fan to ask, [[The opposite? You saw someone who shouldn't be there?]]

Yet another nod. "Those guards must be able to see everything."

Before they could continue, the waiting room door opened and Count Li entered, asking, "Guards? Oh, you mean on the Imperial City?" He gazed at them with a distant air, as if amused by something, and added to someone behind him, "You should be more careful."

"Heh. Sorry about that. Wouldn't be a problem with most, but Book Hunters got good eyes." Pang Hua entered behind Count Li, grinning broadly at them as he pulled the black silk kerchief from his face. "Sorry 'bout that, kid. Didn't want you makin' a scene."

The sight of the bandit chief, combined with his admission that he'd been the one to set that spell on Qing, made Xinglu react before either his master or Master Zhi could stop him. Three long steps took him past Count Li. One sharp grab dragged Pang Hua into the room and twisted him down to the floor.

"TAKE IT OFF QING THIS MINUTE!"

"Now child...."

"Xinglu, stop it right now!"

It was Qing, catching his best friend's wrist and tugging, that made the other boy quiet. "Don't," Qing pleaded. "He's your Chief Cultivator's guest. You'll get in trouble and I'm not hurt. I promise, I'm not hurt."

Xinglu snarled, glaring down at his captive. Pang Hua wasn't helping either. He laughed like an idiot, unimpressed by Xinglu's immense strength and towering rage.

"He could have killed you!" Xinglu snarled at Qing.

"It was just a geas, Xinglu. Nothing more. You don't have to do this."

Slowly Xinglu released Pang Hua's arm. Slowly he stepped back, just one mistake—his or Pang Hua's—away from attacking again. Or, worse, taking his demon hound form and trying to tear Pang Hua's throat out. Really, sometimes Xinglu could get so overprotective.

Or was there more to it? Qing eyed Pang Hua as he slowly rose to his feet, still chuckling, despite the fading bruise on his wrist. There was something about him that didn't sit right. A feeling of something behind the humorous mask that threatened everything in its reach.

Whatever the feeling was, it faded away, the same way the odd feeling Qing kept getting from Count Li did. It was important but he couldn't put his finger on what it was. Knowing better than to push for understanding, he drew back with Xinglu, behind Masters Zhi and Shen.

Because, dragonling or no, demon fire hound or no, neither he nor Xinglu were old enough, wise enough, nor powerful enough to fight either man.

弟子

Zhi Wenku gazed at Pang Hua. "I figured you for a sorcerer," she said levelly. "Obviously a powerful one, given you placed a geas on my apprentice from such a distance. But I'll have you remove it. Now."

He looked down at her with a horribly annoying grin, still chuckling softly. "Apprentices like to talk too much. Wouldn't you prefer it if I made it stronger? And permanent?" He dropped his country accent, clearly aware that there was no point to it here.

"Do you want to offend the Book Hunter's Society by playing fool games with their members?" she asked in turn. "I may not have the power to stand against you, but Leader Feng might have things to say."

Pang Hua still grinned, "I've already taken it off, ma'am." He played with his mask, pretending to be embarrassed and coquettish, adding, "Wasn't going to hurt the lad. Just didn't want him kicking up a fuss."

Before Zhi Wenku could lose her temper with the damned fool, Shen Wei set his hand on her arm, reminding her of her own manners. Bad enough for Xinglu to have lost his temper. Far worse for Zhi Wenku to do so. "Just remember to keep your hands, and spells, off what's under my protection."

That made Count Li chuckle. "I've only known you for a few hours, Master Zhi, but I've this odd feeling you include more than your dragonling apprentice here in that category." He drifted past them to sit behind the desk. "Pang Hua went to investigate something for us. I expect you have something to report too?"

Shen Wei took over, gesturing for the boys to get back and out of the way. "The Pot of Ten Thousand Crows does appear to be the source of the fire crows."

"Only appears?"

"Yes. You know I hate absolutes, sir. Master Tang showed us a few inches of the pot's bottom. Master Zhi confirms the writing is what's described on the pot. As for how those bandits came to acquire it and who put it in their heads to open it where they did? That's not something I can answer."

They turned to Pang Hua, who rolled his eyes and stared off at nothing as if he'd no idea what they were thinking. "The Black Boulder Gang is large and undisciplined. I like it that way but it does mean I don't always know what my people are up to."

"Is this the case now?" Zhi Wenku demanded, when no one else did.

"While it is, I offer no oath to the fact. I'm a known liar and no one believes me except my charmingly elegant and beautiful brother here." Pang Hua bowed in Count Li's direction. To Zhi Wenku's surprise, the Chief Cultivator merely bowed back gracefully.

Pang Hua continued, "The group who were killed were all recent members who'd barely earned their way to second ring in the gang. They were neither terribly smart nor patient. Easy pickings for someone needing them to break my rules and do something really damned stupid."

By which Zhi Wenku supposed the rules involved not taking jobs without permission and not attempting thefts in places like the Imperial Treasury. When she said as much, though, Pang Hua shook his head. "Not the treasury. I was just there, checking the forbidden vault. According to their records, the pot secured there is a copy, created by Emperor Kang Huang's apprentice, Pan Wei."

Someone had made a copy of the Pot of Ten Thousand Crows? If it weren't for her long and weary experience with human hubris, Zhi Wenku would have been shocked. Instead she asked, "So it's gone?"

"Hate to inform you, because I really was hoping there was only the one, but it was right where it belonged, untouched. I even asked it to make sure it hadn't been taken and put back."

Zhi Wenku blinked. "You. Asked. It?"

"Now, Master Zhi, you know as well as I that high order artifacts all got minds of their own. Some can even be human if they like. You should see Miss Windfan when she decides to play." His hands moved as if stroking around something, which made Count Li flick him with a bit of *qi*. "OW!"

"Don't be rude. I don't want her finding out and beating us both again."

"Yeah. I know. Sorry." Pang Hua sighed. "The point is, unless that pot lied to me and I don't think it did, the thing my poor damned fools got hold of wasn't that one. Except...."

"Except it's close enough to do something similar," Shen Wei said, fan displaying the words, [[Deep in the cesspit now.]]

Count Li ignored Shen Wei's resigned complaint. "Master Zhi, I think you can tell that we have quite a problem here." At her agreement, he continued, "My brother and I are bound by certain rules and there are things we aren't allowed to interfere with. Purely human laws and human magics are, unfortunately, among them."

That meant he couldn't take a direct hand in the situation. "I'm wondering why you're telling me this," Zhi Wenku answered, though she had a guess.

"The Soul Protection Society doesn't have an investigator as knowledgeable of artifacts as you are. Could I ask you to take over this investigation? We'll do everything in our power to assist you, but you would have greater leeway than we do to act."

Tell the truth, Zhi Wenku had wondered why Count Li had accepted her presence and her constant nosiness so readily. It was something of a relief, knowing her input would be not only valued but acknowledged without argument. "I can look into it. I make no promises of success."

"Which is about all we have a right to ask of you," Count Li told her.

"Then I agree." A moment's thought determined Zhi Wenku's first steps. "I need to know more about this Pan Wei you mentioned." She knew the general details of local history. She obviously needed to know more.

"Mm. Yes." Count Li agreed. "It begins around two hundred years ago, with Kang Huang, an artificer of some talent and skill, creating powerful, near perfect, replicas of ancient artifacts. The Pot of Ten Thousand Crows, the Puppet Master, the Flame Sword, the Exquisite Pagoda—just to name a few."

Every one of those items were engraved in Zhi Wenku's memory. "Almost all of which were created by the Gods and not intended for mortal hands. Surely he wouldn't have been permitted to continue."

"He wasn't." Count Li indicated himself and Pang Hua. "Our lord and master sent us to stop him. And a hundred and fifty years ago, we did so and destroyed his creations. Except his disciple—Pan Wei—had made his own copies in the course of his training."

"Pan Wei's copies weren't nearly as powerful as Kang Huang's," Pang Hua added. "As such, we weren't allowed to break into the Imperial Treasury to destroy them. They belonged to the mortal world and we'd have had to overstep our bounds to do so."

That really wasn't a surprise. Servants of the Gods had strict rules about what they could and couldn't do. Count Li founding the Soul Protection Society may have pushed those rules already. "Kang Huang is, I presume, dead. Did Pan Wei try to avenge him?"

"No. He'd been forced to follow Kang Huang's orders and was relieved to be free of them. He established an artificer's colony on a mountain northeast of here—Fenghua Shan—and took two apprentices, Zhan Ping and Kang Daoping, Kang Huang's daughter. It was she who created the next problem."

Kang Daoping was the one who'd taken the throne from her brother. The youngest of Kang Huang's many children, her ascent and rule had been bloody and troubled. "Empress Daoping? She was an artificer like Kang Huang?"

"Not his match, but she did copy the Five Color Brush. I've no doubt you know what that is."

Of course she did. The Five Color Brush was an artifact that allowed the user to create images that could come alive. When Zhi Wenku quoted her book, however, Count Li told her, "Being a copy of a copy, Daoping's had a different effect. It seemed to change reality to match what it wrote."

Oh. Oh dear. "That's horrifying."

"It needed a great deal of *qi* to use and a specialized ink. It also couldn't affect high level cultivators like Pang Hua and myself. Unfortunately, it was strong enough to do a great deal of damage. She changed things so she became

Empress. She brought down everyone she thought of as enemies, including her master Pan Wei."

"He had two apprentices. Daoping is gone, of course, but is Zhan Ping still alive?"

"She lives in Chang'an," Pang Hua told her. "In her family's mansion on the south-east side of town."

"I'll pay her a visit tomorrow, then." Another thought occurred to Zhi Wenku. "Pan Wei's work might have been confiscated after his execution. Do you think there'd be records on the subject still?"

Count Li considered that. "There could be? I don't know for certain. But I believe I can get you into the government archives, if that'd help?"

It probably would. If nothing else, it was research and that was what Book Hunters were best at.

CHAPTER 4
A Complicated Investigation

The next morning, after a good night's rest, they all met with Count Li to discuss their plans. As Master Zhi had agreed to take charge, her first statement was, "We have two tasks at hand: speaking with Master Zhan and examining the court records for the time period when Master Pan Wei died."

Count Li agreed, giving her a jade token for the archives. To Qing's surprise she handed it to him. "I should be the one to talk to Master Zhan. You, Xinglu and Shen Wei can research the past."

Since talking to a total stranger who might be behind the recent attack was the last thing Qing wanted to do, he gladly accepted the task. Except, "Will they let me in?"

"I've already spoken to the Archival Secretary," Count Li reassured him. "You won't be allowed near the more recent records, but anything from Daoping's reign is in the historical archives and unimportant to the present government."

Master Zhi continued, "Master Li, will you introduce me to Master Zhan? It might be easier to get answers from her with you present."

Uncertainly, Master Li told her, "Pang Hua and I will come, for curiosity's sake if nothing else, but I'm not sure our presence will help you much. She still blames us for her master's death."

Master Zhi raised a brow. "Any particular reason why?"

"She believes my being mostly immune to the effects of the Five Color Brush meant I could have stopped Daoping from using it against Pan Wei." A slight, rueful, shrug. "I would have tried, but by the time I realized what Daoping was doing, the damage was done. Daoping was enthroned, Zhan Ping was crippled and Pan Wei was beheaded at the gates to his own craft hall. I wasn't permitted to do more than help take Daoping down."

That was a terrible situation and Qing wished he understood more about the matter. He only knew a little about the Five Color Brush and since the one Daoping created appeared to have different powers entirely, there wasn't much more he could guess at.

"I have a general idea of the time period I should be researching," Qing said. "But is there anything specific to look for?"

"Search for any records of Empress Daoping's doings," Master Zhi ordered. "Specifically from the time just before and just after her ascent. See if there's anything left of her own writings. She may have used a personal code for whatever changes she made with the brush, so search for that sort of thing."

"The ink was made from five different flowers," Count Li added. "And characters written with it shift in colors between red to yellow to green to grey to black. If you see that, be careful."

The colors matched the five elements, or close enough. "Do you have any examples?"

"No. We destroyed everything we found, but it didn't do much good."

It seemed unlikely Qing and his companions would find much of use in the records. Still, he knew his Master Zhi's opinion on the subject. Sometimes the smallest piece of information could prove the difference between finding the truth and leaving it to float down the river like a dead leaf.

And part of his job as a Book Hunter was searching through records and archives for the closest thing to the truth possible.

弟子

That Count Li wanted his brother along for their investigation was a bit surprising. At a guess, he was concerned that if Master Zhan was behind the fire yesterday, she might be too strong for Zhi Wenku to handle. He might be right. Zhi Wenku's skills focused on gathering information and making sense of it, not fighting.

As they approached Zhan Ping's home, Zhi Wenku noticed how the fire damage faded the closer they came. She'd have thought it was just because they'd come to its edge, but that wasn't it. She gestured. "Is it just me, or does it look like the fire went around this area?"

Count Li, looking particularly out of place with his pale silks and fall of

"ANY PARTICULAR REASON WHY?"

thick white hair, examined the burn damage thoughtfully. "It isn't just you, Master Zhi."

"Was that boy of Shen Wei's here?" Pang Hua asked, hands behind his head as he sauntered cheerfully beside them. "Maybe he ate the fire."

"It's possible, I suppose. Shen Wei focused their attention on the center of the fire, and that started further south from us, on the other side this area."

Zhi Wenku visualized the city as she'd flown over it the day before. The fire crows had landed just inside the walls, heading for the nearest structures possible. That suggested their controller's orders had been to fly straight to Chang'an and start burning whatever they saw first.

She focused on the mental image and frowned. She'd been too concerned for her wayward apprentice to notice then, but she realized something now. "When I flew over yesterday this part of the city was completely surrounded in flame, in a perfect circle around one clear area."

That made the two men accompanying her stop and raise their brows in near perfect unison. "My good woman," Count Li said. "You didn't think to mention this?"

"I was focused on my apprentice at the time and only just looked at the memory again."

"That's a Book Hunter skill, right? Being able to see a whole memory like it was right in front of you?" Pang Hua asked, sounding interested. "A good ability for someone in your line of work."

Book Hunters cultivated the skill for that very reason. One never knew when one might find a book one couldn't acquire but needed a copy of. Zhi Wenku waved off the compliment. "The center of the unburned area was just ahead of us. Does that house happen to be Zhan Ping's?"

Count Li agreed. "I'll let you take the lead now," he told her. "Zhan Ping won't refuse me entry, but I'd rather she didn't lose her temper because I'm there."

"Now, hey, she isn't terribly fond of me either, you know."

"I wonder why."

Ignoring the pair genially arguing behind her, Zhi Wenku eyed Zhan Ping's house. There were a fair number of homes on this fairly crowded street, but this particular one was unusual in that it was surrounded by a white stone wall. If it'd been on the west side of the city, where the nobles and merchant families lived, its separation would have been perfectly normal. Here amid crowded buildings stuck together in a haphazard fashion, it didn't fit at all.

"Isn't this a bit extravagant for the area?"

"This section used to be better off," Count Li explained. "Time erodes all things, I fear. I believe the Zhan were quite well off once. And Zhan Ping is the last surviving member of the family."

Walking through the great wooden doors leading into the Zhan's outer courtyard, Zhi Wenku was charmed by the little mechanical statues of wood and stone. Shaped like human adults, they were barely four feet tall and designed to look like servants. They each had chores; sweeping the courtyard of leaves and detritus, trimming the trees of dead branches, repairing the paper windows, just to name a few.

"Didn't you say Zhan Ping was an artificer? These look more like a mechanist's work," she said as they entered.

"Artificers and mechanists go hand in hand," an elderly voice said from the side of the courtyard. A woman, sitting in a chair watching her mechanical servants work, a mechanical cat in her lap, a huge mechanical dog just rising to growl at the intruders. "Who said you could come wandering into my home like guests, Mister high and mighty Chief Cultivator? Not to mention bring a stranger and that troublemaking brat of a brother along?"

Zhi Wenku walked closer, unintimidated despite the size of the dog facing her down, gazing levelly at it as it blocked her path. Before anyone could speak, the dog sniffed the air and glared at Pang Hua. With a growl of pure fury, it leapt at the dark-clad man, rushing at him so fast that all Pang Hua could do was leap out of its way and run behind a tree.

As the dog and man rushed back and forth, one barking furiously, the other shouting in a foolish way, Count Li sighed. "Again?" was all he murmured, going to his brother's aid. Now all three ran around like idiots.

Zhi Wenku ignored the fuss. Examined Zhan Ping carefully. Decided on her approach.

Old but not ancient, hair just turning the color of ash. If Zhan Ping was Pan Wei's oldest apprentice she'd be well past a hundred and fifty years at the very least. So, cultivated, but not to the point of Eternal Youth. Possibly the death of her master had something to do with that? Heart demons caused by loss weren't uncommon.

The woman was missing one arm. It'd been replaced by an elegant piece of artifice in the same wood and stone as the mechanisms surrounding them, so Zhi Wenku doubted its loss had stopped her for long. From her features, she didn't smile much but she also didn't look like poor temper had twisted her entirely.

Zhi Wenku cupped her hands lightly, as an elder to a younger. For one thing, she doubted the woman was nearly her age. For another, she wanted to see the woman's reaction. No surprise Zhan Ping's lips went thin and tight. "None of that nonsense from you, missy. Who are you and what do you want?"

So. Old. Cultivated. Not cultivated enough to sense another's strength. Zhi

Wenku straightened, gazing directly into the woman's eyes. "This Zhi Wenku is a Master of the Book Hunter's Sect. I'm assisting the investigation into yesterday's fire."

A sharp and angry, "HAH!" Behind Zhi Wenku, the dog headed for her, only to be blocked by Count Li leaping lightly into its path, spinning his parasol between himself and the enraged puppet. Pang Hua distracted the dog next as he ran towards the other side of the courtyard.

Another sigh. Another bow, this one even less polite than the first. "Master Zhan...."

"Don't play games, little girl!" Zhan Ping snapped, "Book Hunters don't care about fires that don't threaten their libraries."

"They care about fires created by ancient and dangerous artifacts," Zhi Wenku said in turn. "Or, rather, copies of ancient and dangerous artifacts like the Pot of Ten Thousand Crows."

That had the desired effect. Zhan Ping's lips tightened, holding in her reaction. Then, "Stoney. Down boy. Sit."

Stoney obeyed instantly, so that the two men who'd been keeping him entertained could walk away without being bitten on their aggravating asses. As they approached, Zhan Ping gave them disgusted looks and finally said, "There weren't many could create such a thing and they're either dead or lost their cultivation. It seems, maybe, we'd better talk after all."

Standing wearily, not bothering to make sure they followed, Zhan Pin led them inside her house.

弟子

Entering the government's archives was simple, thanks to Count Li's jade token. Entering the required records room took a bit more effort, mostly because Captain Li was in the same section as they meant to examine. "What business does the Soul Protection Society have in the archives?"

Master Shen bowed politely. "Captain Li, this Master and his companions seek information related to the deaths of those bandits from the Black Boulder Gang." He fanned himself lightly while Qing peered past him at the rows of tall dark wooden cabinets filling the dimly lit chamber. So much knowledge.

"That doesn't answer the question." Captain Li glared at Master Shen, stepping closer so his tall form blocked Qing's view of the room. "The Soul Protection Society has no business poking around in government documents, no matter how old."

Qing stood tiptoed so he could see past Captain Li, noting a large table of pale wood, lit by a single flickering lantern overhead. Was that a scroll on top? He needed Master Zhi's talent for distance reading here.

At the same time, Master Shen continued, "Some of what we've learned suggests those bandits' deaths had something to do with the fire...."

"You think they set the fire, then? Pretty quick conclusion, given they're nothing more than rogues and troublemakers."

"Big bro, you said there was a link yourself," a new voice said from among the rows of cabinets. Qing recognized the speaker immediately, one of the two who'd helped capture that scroll from the Count's mansion yesterday. Li Aiqing.

"I don't know how there can be." That was the other guard, what was his name again? Oh, yes, Kang Qiyun. "I mean that pot's still where it belongs."

"Can't you two be quiet," Captain Li grumbled. "Just for once?"

Xinglu snorted. "Good luck with that. They never are."

"Yeah. We never.... Hey!"

"Actually, he's right. We do argue a lot, you know."

"Still, that was mean."

Qing refused to give the pair any extra reason to interrupt. He focused his attention, his widest eyes, and his most foolish expression, on Captain Li. "How'd you find out there might be something important here, Captain?"

The captain eyed him dourly. "You're that dragon, I mean dragonling, aren't you? What are you doing, serving a human like that Book Hunter?"

Qing shook his head. "This Qing is Master Zhi's apprentice," he corrected. "Not her servant. And she's much older and more cultivated than I am."

That made Captain Li blink. He strolled closer, eying Qing suspiciously, then turned to look at Master Shen. "I could ask his question of you. What made you come here?"

Amused, Master Shen murmured, "This could go for a while if we continue to be stubborn." The image of two oxen trying to push the other off a trail formed on his fan. "I shall explain first and trust you'll realize we're best off comparing notes, not hiding truths from each other."

Xinglu snorted and Qing glared at him. "No fire," he muttered in his best friend's ear. "Keep the smoke to yourself. This is a records room."

As Xinglu gave Qing a hangdog look, Captain Li suddenly laughed, expression softening. "It seems your companions are as bad as mine, Master Shen." He spread his hands, adding, "You said you'd explain?"

"You were told about the bodies we found?" At Captain Li's agreement, Master Shen continued, "We believe they got their hands on a counterfeit artifact. One capable of causing the fire yesterday. I've no idea how it came into their hands but the artifact may have belonged to Empress Daoping. We hope to find some record of it here."

Captain Li considered that. "Interesting." He led them to the table at the center of the room, where a large piece of paper with a set of dates and a list of items lay. "This is from the Imperial Treasury's records. We had a break-in last night and someone left a scroll from a hundred and fifty years ago out and open to the information on this page." He indicated the paper.

The writing was an old form of short-hand but one Qing had already learned. "The Gold and Silver Banana Leaf Fan. An Ocean Calming Pearl. The Scroll of Godly Coronation... that has to be a counterfeit...."

"Why?"

"Because the original is with the Book Hunters." The scroll was, after all, the most valuable and powerful of all the Ancient Works. He also didn't like to travel.

From behind the stacks, Kang Qiyun asked, "Book Hunters? That group your master's with?"

"Yes."

"Do you have copies? I've always wanted to read that one."

"Would you stop interrupting?" Captain Li answered before Qing could tell him no. "Keep reading, Apprentice Qing, since you can make that thing out better."

Qing continued, "Fire Washed Cloth, Pot...." He stopped. Took a breath. "The Pot of Ten Thousand Crows. Oh."

"It isn't really a surprise," Master Shen murmured. "We knew Pan Wei's copy was in the treasury."

Came to that, it wasn't surprising the record had been left out. Pang Hua must have done so, possibly—no, certainly—deliberately. "There's just so many artifacts. Why did he copy so many?"

"Copies?" Captain Li demanded. "They're supposed to be original."

"According to Count Li, they're copies created by Kang Huang's apprentice, Pan Wei," Master Shen told him. "I'm guessing you figured out that the fire might have something to do with the Pot?"

"I did. And since it was where it belonged, I came here hoping to find out if there was anything in the records from the time."

An understandable desire. "We don't know the answer to that. But we hope to find out something about the artificers who might have created the thing," Qing told him. "Maybe we should work together?"

Kang Qiyun said, "It sounds like a splendid idea. I'd love to work with a dragon... dragonling."

Now that was embarrassing, especially given the admiration in the young man's voice. Qing wasn't used to that sort of reaction. To his relief, Captain Li said, "Don't be obnoxious. Master Zhi warned us not to treat him like an idol." He turned his attention on Master Shen. "I agree. We should work together. The shelves for Daoping's reign are all over on this side. I'll let you decide where to start."

Master Shen tilted an inquiring brow at Qing, who thought about it carefully. "We'll search for anything related to Pan Wei's execution. You keep looking for whatever artifacts he and his apprentices created. Kang Huang, too, if you find anything."

To Qing's pleasure, all three men agreed without argument and set to searching.

弟子

The inside of Zhan Ping's house had as many wood and stone servants as outside. Some dusted. Some swept. Still others carried things to and fro in a way Zhi Wenku couldn't help but think unnecessary. Noticing her expression, Zhan Ping shrugged. "They're designed to work whenever they're awake. My cultivation's weak, so it's easier to just let them keep going, rather than restart them when I need something done."

It was an unwilling admission of weakness. One Zhi Wenku understood entirely and chose not to acknowledge. "I take it the dolls gather ambient *qi* to continue operating?"

"They're powered by spirit stones." There was a challenging expression in Zhan Ping's eyes, as if she expected Zhi Wenku to decry the extravagance. When she didn't, the woman continued, "You said you're a Master Book Hunter. And you speak as if you're a great deal older than me. What cultivation?"

Truthfully, Zhi Wenku told her, "We don't measure things the same way you would." Book Hunters depended on knowledge, rather than spiritual or magical energy.

"Oh." The woman fell silent as she led them into a small sitting room. "Bring us tea," she told the servant sorting the books in the shelf on the wall. "Quickly."

A tiny curtsy, strange to see on a being whose clothes were literally part of her body and equally solid. Then the puppet hurried off, returning quickly, a large tray of cups and one pot whose contents steamed softly, its flowery scent rising in the air.

Sipping politely, Count Li asked, "Having allowed us to enter, I presume you're willing to discuss matters?"

The old woman gazed silently into her cup, lips tight. Then, "My master died for lack of your support, Master Li."

The Count inclined his head. "This Master is aware and agrees."

"I see no reason why I should help you."

"And yet you haven't sent us packing the way you have in the past."

A scoff. "I allowed this Zhi Wenku in. You just happened to be with her."

Somehow, Zhi Wenku kept her patience, sipping her tea, waving her fan slowly in front of her, waiting for her host to make up her mind. When it was clear Zhan Ping wouldn't talk without encouragement, she said, "Your master created a copy of the Pot of Ten Thousand Crows. Did anyone else?" She avoided mentioning Daoping's name, certain Zhan Ping wouldn't like hearing it.

Proving her right, Zhan Ping scowled. "The brat made a copy, even though master discouraged it. He said it'd get us in trouble with the Society." She turned a dour look on Count Li, adding, "As if you paid any attention to what she was doing."

Count Li gazed at his tea, clearly trying to remain calm about the matter, equally clearly failing. "I had no business interfering with her taking power, you realize?"

"Even so...."

"Even so, I am neither omnipotent, nor omniscient, no matter how cultivated I am." Count Li gave her a long and thoughtful look. "The responsibility for what Daoping created lies with her master and herself."

Zhan Ping retorted. "More powerful and wiser heads could have paid attention to the danger."

It seemed to Zhi Wenku that the woman was doing her best to shame Count Li for his failure to protect and save Pan Wei. As the man's first apprentice, she supposed Zhan Ping had reason to be angry, but there seemed to be a great deal more behind her manner than just that.

Pang Hua noted, "The Soul Protection Society doesn't interfere with human governments. It wouldn't have been their business."

"We probably should have, given how Daoping gained power," Count Li sighed. "I'm more concerned by the existence of that second pot. It probably caused the fire yesterday."

Thin and weathered lips tightened against Zhan Ping's emotions. Then, "This artificer is aware. Equally aware of why it was used."

When the woman fell silent, clearly not wanting to explain more, not wanting to admit more, Zhi Wenku offered, "The culprit meant it for you. As a warning? "

"As if it would work."

There was another possibility. "Your house was protected from the fire. Perhaps the real reason was to find out if you had some means to block the counterfeit's flames? Do you have a way to block the flames?"

Zhi Wenku's question startled the woman. "I... have what little I could salvage of my master's belongings," she admitted slowly. "It's possible. But he never mentioned such a thing to me. I don't remember him mentioning such a thing to me."

Count Li set his teacup down. "Would you allow us to see what you have left?" At her dark expression, he added, "It'd go a long way towards easing my mind regarding your intentions towards the Soul Protection Society, not to mention help prove you aren't involved in this matter."

This was the first time since Zhi Wenku had met the man that he'd behaved like a true official, rather than a slightly fatuous dilettante. She wasn't surprised, having dealt with such people frequently in the past. Too, it seemed to her that Zhan Ping had been giving the man ample cause to be suspicious.

"Why the hell would you think I'm involved? I'm crippled physically and spiritually, thanks to the brat. I didn't know where that damned pot was hidden. I couldn't take it up into the mountain. I certainly couldn't have used my cultivation to release its power."

Before Zhi Wenku could answer, she noted movement. Puppets, six or more of them, thin bodies bending as they passed the doorway, clacking softly with every step. She didn't know who'd created them, nor why they were there, but she was certain of one thing.

They meant no one any good.

弟子

The archive was about the size of a single room of Master Zhi's Warehouse. It was also crammed full of cabinets, making it difficult for Xinglu to move through. Qing, being smaller, had no trouble finding the section detailing the last days of the Kang Dynasty.

"How are you even reading this?" Xinglu grumbled as Qing scanned different scrolls and handed him the ones he thought had important information. "The ink's barely legible and I've never seen half these characters."

"I'm a Book Hunter," Qing reminded him. "We're trained for this sort of thing." He pointed at his eyes, adding, "It's part of our cultivation. I can see the difference between ink intentionally used and ink that's been spilled, too."

"Hey, that's a useful trick," Kang Qiyun called out from his side of the room. "Aiqing-bro here is always spilling ink on his work when he writes reports."

"It took me five years to learn it."

"Five?" That was Li Aiqing, sounding incredulous. "You're just a kid."

"For one thing, he's a dragon, so you don't know how old he is. For another, cultivators start early."

"Oh, yes. Like you know anything about cultivation."

"My illustrious ancestor was a cultivator. And hasn't your uncle been teaching me?"

"Your illustrious ancestor has been dead for a hundred and fifty years. And Uncle Li's just humoring you."

"Could you two work without talking?" Captain Li demanded, pausing his discussions with Master Shen. The two of them had been going over the list of artifacts and trying to work out just how they'd come into Kang Huang's hands.

A thought occurred to Qing. "Was that illustrious ancestor of yours Kang Huang?"

"Yeah! That's him. First Emperor of the Kang Dynasty, such as it was. Hey, I'd be a prince, or something, if Daoping hadn't usurped the throne and ruined the whole thing. I might even be Emperor!"

Captain Li snapped, "Does your mouth ever stop moving, Kang Qiyun? Talk less, search more! Unless you want to tell everybody your business."

By now Qing had found the scroll associated with Pan Wei's case. The artificer had been accused of hoarding valuable artifacts and mechanisms in his craft hall and plotting against Daoping's rule. He hadn't even been brought to trial, just beheaded and left to rot. An unpleasant end, and one that must have been all the worse for being his own student's doing.

Something flickered at the edge of Qing's awareness. A faint surge of *qi*? Or, no, not quite. The difference between ink and the marks it left behind. He scanned the cabinet and spotted the source; a silk scroll clumsily rolled up and shoved too far back beneath the other scrolls to easily remove.

Suspicious, because that was the sort of thing he'd been taught to watch for; Qing worked the scroll out of its hiding place and brought it to the table to look at properly. "The paper's awfully thick," he muttered.

Master Shen fingered the edge. "Paper thickness varied more back then, though. I remember having to double thin sheets up so the ink wouldn't soak through."

No surprise Master Shen was that old. He'd never boasted about his cultivation but he was a capable alchemist and some of their earliest pills were intended to maintain youth and health. Qing grinned at him, unable to resist saying, "You don't look a day over sixty... Unka Master Shen."

"I don't look a day over twenty-five, youngling." Master Shen tapped his skull with his closed fan before adding, "I think you're right, though. For one thing, this is parchment, not paper. It shouldn't be this thick. For another, the page appears doubled and poorly glued back. See here?"

Qing pulled out a paper cutting knife from his sleeve and looked at Captain Li. "May I?"

A sigh. "If you must. Just a corner, unless there's reason to do more. A good thing these records are so old no one will care."

Master Zhi would care if Qing ruined a record, but he thought she'd understand. Sometimes one had to poke around to make sure one got everything. "Xinglu, hold the scroll steady, would you?"

The paper cutting knife was sharper than the sharpest razor, its blade so thin it had to be held carefully and steadily to keep it from bending out of shape. It was also the best tool for this job, allowing the wielder to cut a page in half along its edge. A truly skilled Book Hunter—like Master Zhi—could turn one page into four.

Cutting along the line of glue revealed the page's secret almost immediately. As Qing had thought, there were two pages. One mostly normal thickness, the other thin and light, hidden behind the other. For a moment it seemed that page was just a filler intended to keep ink from seeping through. Except the ink revealed wasn't blotted. Rather it seemed to shift in colors, going from red to yellow to green to grey to black as Qing watched.

"That's the Five Color Brush's work," Xinglu said grimly.

"We need to see the rest of it." Master Shen turned his attention on Captain Li. "You wouldn't know of it, but the Five Color Brush was part of how Daoping took power. Most of her writings were destroyed. If this is something she left behind, we need to know."

Captain Li's expression was cold. "I can't...."

Whatever he was about to say was cut off by the sudden entrance of a Kirin Guard. "Captain," the man said, snapping to attention and ignoring all the strangers, "There's another fire!"

"Mm. Where?"

"Same as yesterday. Except this time it's Zhan Ping's place that's burning."

Qing and Xinglu turned to Master Shen with wide and startled eyes. Zhan Ping was the person Count Li, Pang Hua and Master Zhi had gone to meet. If her place was afire did that mean those three were involved?

Before Captain Li could react, Master Shen straightened. "Much as I've enjoyed this. I think we'd best go take a look." Grimly, he pushed straight past the Kirin Guard and headed out the door.

Qing paused long enough to shove the scroll into his *qiankun* sleeve before he followed.

CHAPTER 5
A Consistent Form of Attack

Stoney leapt to his feet, growling and whining at the puppets. If nothing else, it made Zhi Wenku certain the things weren't Zhan Ping's work. The dog obviously didn't recognize the newcomers and didn't want them anywhere near his master.

Zhi Wenku looked the things over. Tall. Thin. Leather connected pieces of wood and covered the framework of their chests. Ivy grew between the joints, acting like tendons. Their heads were small, mostly there for show, and they'd two extra pairs of arms folded close to their bodies. As for clothing? They neither needed nor wore anything because there was nothing to conceal.

Zhan Ping stood, staring startled at the things. "What in the hell? Those are the brat's puppets!"

Interesting. "How can you be sure?"

"Her favorite materials were leather, wood and ivy.... But all her artifacts were destroyed. What the hell is going on here?"

"Several possibilities, Zhan Ping." Count Li took up a position across from his brother, leaving Zhi Wenku to deal with the woman. "You could be using Daoping's puppets for your own purposes. Or someone out there has sent them after you; the one who started yesterday's fire, perhaps?"

Zhi Wenku drew her battle whisk from her sleeve and watched the approaching puppets thoughtfully. They weren't attempting to attack, just blocking the four of them from escaping. "Your house was protected from the fire by some means. Is it an array or an artifact?"

"An artifact," Zhan Ping admitted. "Guarding the whole house."

"And where is it?"

That made Zhan Ping glance sharply at Zhi Wenku. "You really think I'm going to explain that?"

Zhi Wenku noted how the things seemed to be herding them towards the wall and gestured at it. "You may want to reconsider. They're pushing us into a corner."

That made Zhan Ping look around. "My vault," she said, voice falsely calm. "That's the entrance."

"Is that artifact in the vault, then?"

A sharp sigh. "Of course it is. Where else would it be?" Zhan Ping watched the puppets approaching her as if she meant to stand her ground. Except the nearest puppet reached out with its larger primary arms and grabbed her without pausing a second. "PUT ME DOWN!"

The puppet ignored her, slinging her over its shoulder as the others moved closer. One reached for Pang Hua, only to lose its head to his umbrella. At the same time Count Li caught hold of one of the other puppet's wrists and broke off its arm with a delicate little twist.

Damaging the puppets had dangerous consequences. The things fell out of the link with their companions, dropping to the ground as if no longer able to act. For a moment they lay in place, leather-covered chests heaving strangely, only to spasm and twist and shriek. Smoke rose from their injuries, along with gouts of oil-fueled fire that set the furniture alight.

Zhan Ping yelled curses as she struggled to pull free of her captor. "THE HELL ARE YOU DOING?"

Zhi Wenku ignored the woman's fussing, flicking her whisk around the puppet's arms and prying Zhan Ping free. She caught her gently, putting her over her shoulder. "Hold still."

"MY STUDY!"

"Will screaming and cursing save it?" Zhi Wenku asked. She glanced around. Tightened her lips. "Boys," she called, eliciting identically amused glances, "My whisk's water element isn't strong enough for this fire. Can you get us past it?"

"We can block it," Count Li told her. "We can't stop more puppets without breaking them and making things worse."

A good point, except it was already worse. The flames spread fast and the other puppets burned as well, as if that was their primary purpose. The stench of lamp oil grew stronger.

Apparently their enemy intended to force them down a narrow path. Or, rather, they meant to force Zhan Ping down it. If Zhi Wenku and her companions hadn't shown up just before the puppets had, the woman would have been helpless to do anything but flee into her vault.

At a guess, the source of their troubles wanted Zhan Ping's treasures, meaning the last thing they should do was give the enemy a chance at it. They had to escape. The question was, "How can we get out of here?"

Calm, unruffled, Count Li looked at his brother again. The pair seemed to debate silently. Then Count Li drew his parasol and the pair stepped to either side of Zhi Wenku and Zhan Ping.

Silk and metal glittered as the things spun on their axis. The brothers stepped backwards, tight against the two between them. As one, they pulled their umbrellas in and closed the things around them.

A flash of chaos energy half-blinded Zhi Wenku as she felt the familiar surge and jerk of a transportation spell.

弟子

Although only one building was alight, the fire was bigger than Qing expected. Bigger and stinking far worse than the fire crows had. That'd been a natural fire, fueled by wood and textiles. This one stank of lamp oil.

The walls of the building held the flames back but sparks flew overhead, striking the nearby buildings and smoldering there. If the area hadn't already been burned and abandoned, the neighboring homes would have been at risk. Even now there was a chance the whole thing could go up in flames again.

"Master," he whispered, his confidence that Master Zhi could escape and survive pretty much anything shaken. The fire was so big and his master's battle whisk wasn't strong enough for it. Was she all right in there? Surely Count Li and his brother would save her. Even if she couldn't protect herself, they were powerful cultivators, right?

Master Shen set a reassuring hand on Qing's shoulder. "Can you manage another storm?" he asked gently, giving Qing something to do.

"I can't," he denied. "I used up most of my strength on yesterday's fire."

"I can eat it," Xinglu offered. "If you want me to, Master?"

A weary chuckle. "While I'd wish not, given how close the last fire brought you to breakthrough, I'm afraid it's necessary. Go. Be careful."

Xinglu rushed towards the burning building, body shifting as he went, so that by the time he leapt over the stone wall he was a huge black dog breathing smoke and flames.

Qing looked around for something to do himself and saw the city guards and citizens running up to the fire with buckets upon buckets of water. It wouldn't stop the source but they could keep things from spreading. So could he, just like the guards were. He looked pleadingly at Master Shen who nodded, gesturing for him to go.

Running to join the others, Qing found two buckets and followed those fighting the outer edges of the fire. He could move faster as a dragonling. Could carry more buckets, too. But that'd scare everyone, so he wouldn't.

Bucket after bucket filled. Bucket after bucket emptied. Spark after spark rose. And spark after spark sizzled and fizzled to nothing as they soaked the surrounding buildings and doused every flame they could. All while someone inside the old mansion's walls barked and howled with wild abandon.

Kang Qiyun complained as he passed Qing. "That crazy hound's having

"THE WALLS OF THE BUILDING HELD THE FLAMES..."

fun in there. How can he be having fun? This isn't fun. This is a disaster. A tragedy!"

The young man wasn't wrong but he wasn't right, either. "Fire is his element," Qing pointed out. "He can't help enjoying it. And he is doing something to keep it from becoming a bigger tragedy."

Li Aiqing added, "You're just mad because big bro won't let you do more than carry water."

"Am not."

"Are too."

Abandoning the inevitable argument to hurry to another smoldering spot on a nearby roof, leaping up to reach it, Qing paused a moment afterwards to gaze at the fire from above. Xinglu had cleared the outer edges of the fire first, so all that was left was the column of flames rising from the middle of the main building. He frowned, noticing human figures moving quickly around the outer courtyard.

"There's people inside," he called down to Master Shen. "I'll help them!"

The wall wasn't difficult to cross from his position. Qing dropped to the ground in a badly burned garden, where a small man dressed in simple clothes struggled desperately to protect an old and well cared for paulownia tree.

Realizing the young man was alight himself, Qing rushed forward to help, intending to drag the boy away. The tree wasn't worth his life and burning would be a horrible death. Except the boy was unexpectedly heavy. When he turned a pleading gaze on Qing, it became obvious he was a puppet of carved stone and wood.

Now Qing knew he'd thrown himself into danger for unliving beings. He might have rushed off, but something about the puppet's pleading motions made him stop. "Here. You're on fire too. That won't help." He filled his bucket from the nearly emptied pond, glad the koi flopping in the mud were puppets too, and poured it on the boy-puppet.

A silent nod of appreciation. Then the puppet went back to beating out the fire that'd come far too close to that tree. Qing helped, keeping an eye out for other fires and other puppets set alight. These weren't like the ones in Zhu Kan's mountain stronghold. There weren't any true human souls or minds inside their stone skulls. But they clearly had enough awareness to ask for help and he couldn't leave them unaided.

弟子

It was barely possible to see their new location between the edges of the brothers' umbrellas. Not that Zhi Wenku was sorry. She knew where they were and knew the umbrellas protected them from the Chaos outside the world.

This wasn't the time to demand explanations. She doubted she'd get a reasonably honest one, anyway. Count Li seemed quiet and aloof and utterly beyond the sort of behavior his brother obviously embraced, but he was as much a trickster as Pang Hua. Taking anything either brother claimed at face value would always be a mistake.

There was one question. "Why are we here, instead of going somewhere safe?"

"My good woman, you are safe as long as we're here," Count Li told her. At her scoff, he chuckled softly and added, "Neither of us have the power to teleport. Nor do we have any talismans. The best we could do was bring you into this space and wait out the fire. I'm keeping a sense for it, never fear. I'm sure it'll be put out soon enough."

Now it was Zhan Ping's turn to scoff. "And what'll be left of my home, I ask? My poor servants and my poor mansion, ruined because of you three."

An unfair presumption. "The fire wasn't our doing. If anything, we've saved your most valuable possessions from the one who set it."

Silence. Then, "What's that mean?"

"Master Zhan, is the vault fireproof?"

Zhan Ping glared at Zhi Wenku, squeezed close against her shoulder in a most uncomfortable way. "Of course it is! Who builds a vault that can't withstand fire? Hell, if that puppet hadn't exploded in my sitting room the house wouldn't be burning at all!"

"I suspect those puppets are after your vault. Trapped as we were, your only other safety would be to hide inside it."

"Not to be argumentative, but some of us need air to breathe, Master Zhi," Count Li pointed out. "A fireproof vault is surely air-tight. I wouldn't want to think about how hot it'd get in there. I don't fancy myself baked. I'm far too stringy."

"Sliced thin and lightly fried would be better," Pang Hua agreed, to both Zhan Ping and Zhi Wenku's irritation. Sensing his humor had fallen flat, the man continued, "But your point's a good one. Those puppets were designed to burst into flame."

"All of which leaves us with the question of what, exactly, you have that someone wants. Not to mention the question of why they're using Daoping's tools. Did she leave descendants?"

Zhan Ping considered that. "None that I know of. She was too selfish to reproduce. She'd have had to share if she did." Another moment of silence, then, "She did have plenty of sycophants, all wanting the power she could give them. I suppose one might have gotten hold of some of her things. What pretty boy here didn't destroy, that is."

Something shook the umbrellas surrounding them but both brothers held fast and Pang Hua shouted, "Scram, you annoying little hundun! Go look for someone else to play with!"

Hundun were chaos beasts, with no true shape of their own. No surprise they'd be wandering around this place. The surprise was how easily the Count and Pang Hua held them off. "My curiosity rises," Zhi Wenku muttered. "And there's nothing I can do about it."

"You're a clever woman, Book Hunter Zhi, full of so much knowledge of things magical. I'm sure you'll figure something out someday." Count Li reached through the narrow gap and poked the hundun, sending it rushing away with its metaphorical tail between its metaphorical legs. "Please, continue your theory about the current situation."

Zhi Wenku focused on their primary purpose. "You were Pan Wei's senior apprentice. It makes sense that you'd save as much of his possessions as you could after Daoping had him executed. I think you took more than a few things when you escaped."

"You think that rotten brat would have let me get away if she knew I had anything?"

The key word was knew and Zhi Wenku said so. "I think you took as much as you could. I think you hid it before she got to them. The question is, how did you manage to do so when I'm sure she would have used that brush of hers to change things and people to suit her, including you?"

A sigh. "That damned brush didn't change reality. It changed what people thought was real. And she almost got me. If I hadn't used my copy of the Precious Lotus Lantern to block her I would have been just as enslaved to her spell as everyone else."

The original Precious Lotus Lantern was an immensely powerful device that would hold off any monster, spirit or God. Zhi Wenku doubted the copy was that strong, but it must have been good enough to keep the Five Color Brush from changing all of Zhan Ping's memories.

Count Li turned his head to look down at Zhan Ping. "You might have mentioned the matter to me. Particularly the fact that she hadn't truly changed things, just made everyone believe differently. This whole time I thought Pang Hua and I were the only ones who knew what she'd changed."

"Not to mention," Pang Hua added, "if we knew about that lantern, we could have used it to help stop her faster. If you weren't so mad at us for playing along, that was."

It was hard to see Zhan Ping's expression, given how squashed they were against each other, but Zhi Wenku thought the woman flushed with embarrassment. "You wouldn't have been able to use it. It broke while I was escaping. How was I supposed to know, anyway? You didn't destroy her memory change when you were fixing things, so I thought you either couldn't or wouldn't!"

They were getting distracted. The past was important, yes, and some of what Zhan Ping had told them was vital to working out what was actually going on. But right then they needed to know what she had in her vault. Zhi Wenku was about to say as much when it suddenly hit her. "You said you destroyed Daoping's tools and works, but what if there were more copies? Even knowing the truth of what she'd done, would you know where she'd hidden them?"

"I... I don't think I would. As I've pointed out, I'm not all powerful." The Count paused. "The fire's out. We can go back and none too soon. I think we have a great deal to investigate."

The brothers did something with their weapons and once more chaos energy flared and faded, until they stood in the burnt out ruins of Zhan Ping's sitting room again.

This time with a large and anguished hell-hound twisting around on the floor in front of them.

弟子

The flames had finally died down when Xinglu's howls of pain drew Qing's attention. Having no fire left to fight, he nodded to the gardener puppet and rushed inside the ruined building, trying not to choke on the stench of burnt wood, paper and far more lamp oil than was strictly necessary.

He followed the sounds to a room that might have been pleasant once, if it hadn't been charred to unrecognizability. What remained were four human figures and the hell-hound who was Qing's best friend. Xinglu lay on the ground, twisting and struggling against something, cracks running through his body as if he were a thing of pottery just about to shatter.

"Master Zhi!" Qing called out, "What's wrong?"

Count Li answered, "He's having a breakthrough. Drat the child. He should know his limits!" The man dropped to one knee beside Xinglu, hand on the hell-hound's head, sending a flow of calming *qi* through him. "I can't stop it, but I can slow it down. We need to get him somewhere safe."

A breakthrough meant Xinglu had reached his next level of cultivation and with it his tribulation. "This city's had enough fires," he said. "Let me take him."

Master Zhi eyed him dourly. "Such as where?"

Before Qing could ask for suggestions, Count Li murmured, "The pavilion behind my mansion. It's built to take tribulations and *qi* deviations."

Qing turned to his master. "May I?"

"Yes." Zhi Wenku waved her fan at him, "Go. Be quick. That boy can't hold it in much longer."

Qing glanced upwards, making sure enough of the roof had been burned away to let him fly through. He took his dragonling form, causing the fourth person in the room to gasp in wonder. Wasting no time preening, he picked Xinglu up and rose into the air.

There were yells and shouts outside from the people dealing with the last bits of the fire. Controlling the perfectly natural urge to spin in the air in a complicated dance, Qing flew towards Count Li's mansion, scanning the mountain behind for the pavilion.

He found it easily, a large octagonal stone platform, its surface covered in intricate patterns that Qing didn't have time to study. He set Xinglu down at the center and backed away. His best friend's body was already searingly hot, to the point that Qing would have burned himself if he weren't a dragonling. Even now his scales felt mildly singed.

He scanned the area, hoping he didn't have to do anything special to keep Xinglu from burning everything in sight. Thank the Gods there weren't any trees nearby. The pavilion sat atop a stony peak without a trace of green. Marks of previous tribulations darkened the stone in places and there was a boulder off to the side that'd been cleaved in two by a human shape crashing into it.

As Xinglu's body heated to intense red, the platform's carvings lit up, glow changing between all the elemental colors in a coruscating display that reminded Qing of the scroll he'd borrowed from the hall of records. He shoved that thought away, a twinge of guilt tugging at him. Maybe he shouldn't have taken it?

The platform's glow stretched out, reaching the edges within moments, then formed translucent walls that rose high into the air. Four of those walls took on images; this land's Four Cardinal Gods. Chi Guo with his jade pipa, Zeng Zhang with his great sword, Guang Mu with his parasol, and Duo Wen with his golden pagoda.

The other four walls displayed talismanic script, protective symbols and arrays that blocked Xinglu's energies from escaping. They couldn't, or wouldn't, block tribulation lightning. After all, it'd negate the whole reason for a tribulation if the cultivator breaking through didn't face it on their own.

As if thinking about the stuff summoned it, Qing noted the sky just above the pavilion turning grey, darkening to black, purple tinted lightning flowing through the darkness. At the same time Xinglu came to his feet, all four limbs splayed as he struggled to stay upright.

Xinglu howled, one low moan of sound that sent fire blazing around him. Another howl, louder and deeper, set those flames rising higher. A huge cry echoed, louder than the thunder rolling overhead. Now the lightning struck, a single impossibly straight bolt of chaos energy slamming into Xinglu's body, clearly intent on obliterating the one who dared face it as an equal.

More bolts struck and struck and struck. And each time Xinglu howled and howled and howled again, challenging the wind, the storm, the lightning. Qing could hear words in his howls, "I am the wolf of the south, the hound of fire. The blood in my veins is the blood of the earth itself. Strike me as you will, I will not falter and I. Will. Not. Fall!"

Eight bolts struck. Eight times Xinglu almost sprawled. Eight times Xinglu somehow managed to stand. Until, at last, the skies cleared, the protective array faded. Until, at last, all that was left was a shaky young man half-crumpled at the center, his naked body singed and scorched but very much alive.

Qing sighed in relief as he returned to his best friend's side. He'd known how much Xinglu had dreaded this tribulation. Xinglu was only a half-demon, after all, and his cultivation had focused on his human core, rather than his demonic. He'd hoped to raise the latter further, to help him survive the former's rise, but those two fires had pushed him too far.

"Hey." Qing turned human and knelt beside Xinglu. "You have any clothes?"

A weak nod. "...in my ring..." Xinglu rubbed at the black jade wrapped around his forefinger, summoning a pile of dark black fabric.

It was a good thing his friend had a storage device capable of withstanding fire, especially given what'd happened to his clothes. Qing helped Xinglu dress and pulled a steamed roll from his *qiankun* sleeve, adding, "This is the best I can do until we get back. It's not like I expected to have feed you, after all."

Xinglu chuckled, accepting the bread and devouring it in one bite. He was clearly too tired for conversation, so Qing just turned dragonling again, letting his friend sit on his back before flying back to Chang'an. Under ordinary circumstances he'd be more discreet.

This wasn't an ordinary circumstance at all and he wanted to find out what was going on.

CHAPTER 6
Seeking Knowledge

"That... that was a dragon!"

For the first time in the last hour or so, Zhi Wenku felt real humor. "Why do you all act like that? He's barely ascended."

Zhan Ping stared after Qing, even though the boy and his fiery burden were no longer in sight. "A dragon is a dragon, surely."

"Not when they're barely fifty years old." Turning her attention on the room around them, Zhi Wenku noted the badly damaged plaster on the wall concealing the vault. Part of an iron door was just visible amid the wreckage. "I'll introduce you to him when he returns."

That made Zhan Ping turn and look at her with wide eyes. "You can introduce me?"

"She's his master," Count Li told the woman. "He's her apprentice."

Once again a questioning look. "Not your disciple?"

Zhi Wenku rolled her eyes. People outside of Khaitan were a bit too enamored of dragons, thinking even the babies should be given more respect than they'd earned. Though, to be fair, Qing was getting close to the day when she could confirm him as a true disciple.

Firmly, she repeated what she'd told Count Li earlier. "He's a baby. He'll get his discipleship when he's earned it." While Zhan Ping took that information in, Zhi Wenku went to the damaged wall, inspecting it closely without touching it, without even breathing on it. She didn't want to risk setting off any traps.

"You really are older than I am, aren't you?"

With a sigh, Zhi Wenku agreed. "Quite a bit. I am a Master Book Hunter, after all." She didn't bother with specifics. Count Li and Pang Hua were likely her seniors and it wouldn't do to brag. Instead she checked the rest of the room, noting the puppets that'd set fire to the mansion were mostly burned away.

One remained partly unburned but it'd been torn into pieces between two sets of powerful jaws. One of those sets had to have belonged to Xinglu. The rest was Stoney's work; he lay in a corner over the remains, gnawing at the leather with determined purpose.

Zhi Wenku spotted the signs of the fight that'd destroyed the puppet. It ended in that corner, with Xinglu grasping hold of one arm and Stoney the leg it still gnawed. The rest lay scattered across the floor, the shattered head rolled off to the side, leaking some kind of vegetable matter; southern squash, it looked like.

Following the trail of destruction back to the vault wall, she noted that the plaster around the lock had been broken off. At a guess, the puppet had been trying to break in. "I think that one was the leader," she said, pointing at the remains, "Or at least the only one with any intelligence."

Pang Hua picked up the leather covered squash. Bounced it on the palm of his hand like a ball, then set it spinning on his finger. "Because its head wasn't hollow?"

That wasn't Zhi Wenku's reason but perhaps the solid inside had given its creator something to work with? Zhi Wenku shrugged. "I wouldn't know. It just looks like it was trying to get inside the vault before Stoney and Xinglu got to it."

The other three looked at the wall and Zhan Ping said, "It does look like someone was breaking in."

Count Li agreed. "Which suggests its controller wanted something inside."

"You're going to demand I let you in, aren't you?" Zhan Ping sounded wearily inured to the idea. Inured and thoroughly disgruntled. "I can't say you're wrong."

"I can't force you to cooperate," Count Li told her. "Although, it'd be best if you did. The one behind these fires isn't going to...."

The Count's statement was interrupted by a crash at the door. Shen Wei, with Captain Li behind him remonstrating and those two guards from Count Li's mansion a bit behind. "WENKU!"

"My dear man," she said. "I'm safe. Just fine."

He strode towards her, fan out and covered in so many terrified words that she could only make out a few. [[Not burned.]] [[Safe?]] [[Gods!]] [[Sure... dead]]]. To look at his face one might think he felt nothing, that he was merely amused and mildly concerned. To look at the words on his fan, it was obvious he'd been near breaking at the thought of her in danger.

She drew her own fan. Stroked his cheek lightly. Then set the words, [[My dear, I'm completely safe,]] on it, so only he could see. [[No need to fret. Your Chief Cultivator and his brother kept me uncharred and unsmoked.]]

He took several deep breaths, forcing himself to calm. Then, "Am I right thinking Xinglu had a breakthrough?"

"He did. Qing took him to Count Li's pavilion."

"Ooh. Darn! I was hoping to watch the next tribulation up there," Li Aiqing said.

"I was hoping to be the next tribulation up there!" Kang Qiyun added.

"Oh, that'd be even better."

"You're not even close to cultivating to that level, young man," Count

Li sighed. "And would you be quiet before I geas you again? We're busy investigating the fire."

Captain Li bowed to his uncle. "Sir, shall I take them away?"

After a moment of thought, the Count waved off the idea. "Not just yet. I want to talk to you first. Stay here and keep guard while we examine the vault."

To Zhi Wenku's surprise, the order actually pleased Captain Li. Apparently he wanted to be involved just as much as his two young companions did. He nodded briefly and took up a position near what was left of the door.

The Count returned his attention to Zhan Ping. "As I was saying, before we were interrupted, it's obvious someone wants inside your vault. I'd like to find out why. Master Zhan, will you please allow us to investigate?"

Zhan Ping eyed him. Eyed everyone else in the charred remnants of her study. Sighed. "I hate this," she grumbled, going to the vault door and knocking more plaster from its surface. "But you're right, Count Li. Unfortunately."

With that, she fiddled with the workings and pulled the door open.

弟子

Returning to Chang'an and the ruins of that building, Qing fully expected to find his master waiting, or at least somewhere in the area. Instead Captain Li and his two chatterbox companions stood guard in the same room as before, watching over a small iron door.

"They've gone to inspect the vault," Captain Li told Qing when he turned human again. "You're to wait."

"That's not fair," Qing complained. "They couldn't even wait for us to get back?"

Kang Qiyun nodded vociferous agreement. "They wouldn't let us come with them, either. So many interesting things and we don't get to take one look!"

Before Captain Li could scold the younger boy again, the sound of dozens of booted feet rushing towards them drew their attention. As they turned to face the newcomers, Qing was unsurprised to see a squad of well-trained Kirin Guards, led by Commander Fan, marching into the room.

Coming to a halt, Commander Fan eyed them, cold eyes fierce and perhaps a bit angry. "Where's the dragon?"

Qing hesitated. Chose equivocation over honesty. "I don't see a dragon anywhere, sir." After all, he wasn't looking at himself. Instinctively, he tightened his robe a bit, making sure his Royal Blue Koi markings were hidden.

"Nor do I," Xinglu added, quite a bit more dishonestly, his lie echoed by both Kang Qiyun and Li Aiqing. Captain Li didn't bother to answer at all, leaving Commander Fan to assume he agreed.

Qing was going to have to learn the trick of lying someday, because Commander Fan accepted their answers grimly. "The Empress wishes to speak with the thing. Where did it go? Doesn't it have any manners at all?"

Kang Qiyun made a peculiar little squeak, but Qing ignored him, too annoyed at the claim that he didn't have manners. To prove he did, he answered politely, "I really couldn't say, sir. Do you know why her Majesty wants to speak with that person?" He emphasized the word, annoyed at being called a 'thing', as if he were a mere animal.

That made Commander Fan scoff. "Dragons are the Gods' messengers to the Royal Family alone. They don't have any business making storms or flying around without so much as acknowledging that."

Oh dear. It'd never occurred to Qing that the local government would take his very existence that way. "I don't think he's a Heavenly Dragon, Commander. He's not nearly old enough."

"You know the beast?"

"I know him somewhat," Qing admitted, put out at the man's insistence on treating him like a animal. "Not as well as I'd like." Who could really claim to know themselves perfectly, after all? Besides, "He's just a baby, I promise you. Nothing to do with the Gods at all."

A pause, while the Commander eyed him dourly. Then, "Can you speak for the dragon?"

"I... I can try. But I don't understand why...."

It was Xinglu who explained, sighing as he did so. "Dragons, even common dragons like the one earlier, are considered symbols of the Emperor and the Empire. To have one so close and not take the opportunity to commune with them would be unthinkable. Though I don't know why it's the Empress asking for him, instead of the Emperor."

Another odd noise from Kang Qiyun, one Commander Fan spoke over without paying mind. "Not your business. All you need to do is come with me and hear her commands."

Commands? If a Heavenly Dragon did come to Earth to meet the Empress they'd be the one doing the commanding, not her. Qing forced back annoyance. "But my Master might need my help. I can promise to ask the dragon to speak with the Empress later, but I can't just leave."

A filial devotion to duty ought to have made the Commander back off and let Qing go. Instead he spread his hands. "The Empress is insistent. If I can't bring back the dragon, I need to bring you. Since, as you say, you can speak for the creature. Or can at least try."

Qing didn't like the idea. He was tempted to take his true form immediately, fly over to the palace and tell the Empress to stop bothering him. Why were these people so enamored of his kind? It wasn't as if he could grant wishes or transform the kingdom to a paradise.

Was this some sort of trap? Qing wished he had some way to communicate his concern to Xinglu. Maybe the two of them needed special fans as well? Lacking that, he simply sighed, cupping his hands and bowing to the Commander. "This Qing can only agree, though he hopes the Empress won't insist he stay for any length of time."

Thankfully, Xinglu caught on. "Indeed," he said. "I'm sure Empress Ling Fei understands that a word or so is sufficient. Qing and Master Book Hunter Zhi are Chief Cultivator Li's guests, after all. She wouldn't interfere with the duty Count Li owes them."

Commander Fan eyed Xinglu sharply, gaze intent. He obviously picked up on the faint undertone of threat in Xinglu's voice, not to mention the warning that Qing was under Count Li's protection. "I'll make sure he's safe, boy. No need to flap that long tongue of yours.'"

"Of course." A slight bow. "I shall accompany Qing on his visit. He's had no etiquette classes in his life and I don't want him making a mistake and be unintentionally rude."

For a moment Qing feared Commander Fan would refuse. Instead he sighed and agreed. "Come along, then." He turned and walked out of the room, not bothering to make sure they were following him.

"It'll be all right," Kang Qiyun said. "Ling Fei's not so bad. It's Chief Eunuch Zhao you have to watch." He glanced at Captain Li and added, "Besides, the Emperor might take a hand. He wouldn't like the dragon meeting the Empress first."

Qing sighed. He didn't want to go but he didn't dare push his luck with these people. They'd likely drag him to the Empress if he didn't cooperate. Unable to argue, he followed Commander Fan to the Imperial City.

He just hoped this wouldn't turn out a mistake.

弟子

They climbed down several stories worth of rungs to reach Zhan Ping's vault. The ladder well was tight and dusty, covered in cobwebs that would have infuriated anyone in charge of keeping valuables safe and protected. A storage facility didn't need to be the height of cleanliness, but the presence of spiders implied other insects and other insects implied damp and food.

Zhi Wenku didn't complain. This wasn't her vault and the goods inside might not be books. Even if they were, they might be properly protected against whatever pests lurked in this place. She was just glad her Warehouse was tucked away in her *qiankun* sleeve, safe from the elements and discovery.

When they reached the end of the ladder, Zhan Ping led them through a short dark hall to yet another metal door. This one had an elaborate locking system, almost certainly protected by dangerous traps.

If so, Zhan Ping disarmed them too quickly to be noticed. And when she shoved the door open to reveal a long and dimly lit tunnel stretching out both left and right, Shen Wei couldn't help saying, "I do hope you're not leading us in circles."

"Only one circle, Master Shen. Don't worry. This is just part of my vault's protection."

The tunnel did indeed circle back to what seemed like the same door they'd entered by. Except when Zhan Ping opened it, it revealed a small room with no ladder and one more iron door, slightly rusted from disuse. It took both Zhan Ping and Pang Hua to push it open, revealing a brightly lit chamber.

To Zhi Wenku's relief, the cobwebs didn't extend into this hidden place. The room, a bit bigger than Zhan Ping's study, was built of polished grey stone, with shelves along the walls and a few crates stuck between. There were devices and tools and piles of random objects on the shelves, including a stuffed river lizard hanging overhead.

Not being an artificer, Zhi Wenku couldn't guess at their use. Among the objects were an incense burner shaped like a poorly carved turtle; a belt sword, its blade twisted out of shape; a parchment and wood umbrella; a box carved with the Khaitanese character for the west, the intoxicating scent of an old book drifting through the cracks.

This not being the time for Zhi Wenku's personal obsessions, she turned to the next shelf. A badly damaged arm of paper and metal; a small bronze chariot pulled by small kirin, a palm-sized wire and paper umbrella similar to the larger one on the first shelf. "This was Master Pan's work?"

"En. His master had him create copies of dozens of fabled artifacts. That's a prototype," Zhan Ping told her.

The umbrella might imitate Guang Mu's weapon, an artifact capable of connecting reality and chaos. If so, Zhi Wenku doubted it'd worked properly. Great Artifacts didn't copy at all well. She turned her attention on the Count, "Are any of these things particularly important? There's entirely too many for us to play guessing games."

Count Li glanced at Shen Wei with a broadening smile. "I think I see why you like her. So very direct."

Fan fluttering in front of him, Shen Wei set the words [[Don't think about rivalling me, Master Chief Cultivator.]]

That set the pale-haired man laughing softly. "Don't drink vinegar on my account, my boy. I'm not looking for a mate." He returned his attention to Zhi Wenku, "Absent a list of items, I don't see any answer but to examine everything...."

Before he could finish, Zhan Ping spoke up impatiently. "I do keep records, you know."

That should have been their first question. "Show me."

Zhan Ping fetched a large book, its pages formed of thin sheets of pressed bamboo. The first few pages were in a wild hand, legible but terribly disordered.

Count Li smiled wistfully at the writing. "I'd forgotten what organized chaos he was. So brilliant and so impossible."

Zhi Wenku scanned the pages, noting mention of various devices and artifacts. No names, just a brief description of what the thing was and what it could do. The incense burner could bring good dreams. The arm was intended for a friend injured in battle and had never been used. The umbrella was described as a complete failure, 'rain soaks right through'.

She read that one aloud, eliciting chuckles from the brothers, and continued on. The next page was in a much better hand, neat and delicate and very precise. The items mentioned didn't describe their uses, either, suggesting the writer didn't know.

"This is your handwriting?" Zhi Wenku asked Zhan Ping. At the woman's agreement, she continued reading, seeing nothing truly useful. "You don't have any more of Pan Wei's tools or notes, then?"

"Those were all destroyed, along with his craft hall."

That made the Count lift his head and blink at her. "His craft hall wasn't destroyed. I distinctly remember Daoping trying to get in and failing."

"What are you talking about? Of course she got in. I watched her burn everything!" Anger flared in Zhan Ping's voice and expression and Zhi Wenku had to set a hand lightly on the woman's wrist as she stepped towards Count Li.

"That was part of Daoping's workings, Master Zhan," Count Li told her. "You managed to evade much of the Five Color Brush's effects, but it seems you didn't escape it entirely."

"You're talking nonsense!" Zhan Ping pulled free of Zhi Wenku's touch and rushed at him. He evaded her easily.

"Another aspect of that damned artifact of Daoping's," Pang Hua noted as he watched the pair fight. Or, rather, watched Zhan Ping try to fight while Count Li calmly evaded her. "Those it affects have a great deal of trouble accepting the truth when it conflicts with the brush's falsehood."

That wasn't good. "Shen Wei?"

"Of course, my dear." Shen Wei reached into his sleeve and pulled out a small snuff bottle, dumping a pinch or so of its contents into his palm. "Master Zhan, my apologies."

Stepping closer, he fanned the powder in her face, rocking her back a step or so. She shook her head like a bull who'd found something heavier and harder than their own skull. Then she dropped into a sitting position, moaning softly.

"I broke the brush. Destroyed her ink. Burned every one of Daoping's writings I could find. I just can't seem to do a thing about the harm she did," Count Li mourned.

Zhi Wenku considered that. "Master Zhan knows the brush's power. Remembers some of the truth. We should try again later, when she's in a better state of mind."

"There's still the question of what, exactly, the person behind those fires intends," Shen Wei pointed out. "They've gone to a lot of trouble and drawn a great deal of attention to themselves. Either they're up to something elsewhere, or Master Zhan is keeping something important to them here."

Zhi Wenku considered that. Continued scanning Zhan Ping's records. "This is interesting," she said suddenly.

"Hm?" Count Li was playing with the little mechanical parasol, chuckling at the way it opened and folded itself into a crane shape. "What is it?"

"There's something not mentioned in the records." She took the object from its silk-lined box, examining it carefully, trying to work out just what it was. Not an artifact; she couldn't sense any *qi* in it at all. Not a device, either. Just a pronged hair stick of pure white jade, a white rabbit carved at one end.

"Hm? Oh, that was Pan Wei's favorite hair stick. I never saw him without it. Master Zhan must have acquired it after he was executed."

Zhi Wenku examined the stick carefully, fingers sliding across the smooth surface. No. Wait. Not entirely smooth. There were tiny words carved between the prongs, just readable thanks to Zhi Wenku's special vision. She focused on them, saying, "Rooster, snake, tiger, rat, goat."

"Eh?"

She waved the question off, checking the other prong. "Earth, metal, wood, water, fire." Further investigation revealed small indentations at the thickest end of the prongs, towards the top of the hair stick. They were too irregular to be mere design and she pointed to them, saying as much.

Pang Hua took the thing from her, brows furrowed. "Pan Wei claimed this was the key to everything."

Count Li added, "He locked up his craft hall when he realized Daoping meant to harm him. We never have figured out how to get in, but the door is just covered in carvings. I believe every beast of the zodiac was included."

Handing the stick back to Zhi Wenku, Pang Hua told her, "You'd best hold onto this."

Zhi Wenku accepted it, understanding why he'd given it to her. There was a good chance it was what the arsonist wanted from Zhan Ping. If so, the last place they'd expect it to be hidden would be on an outsider like Zhi Wenku. She set it in her *qiankun* sleeve, planning to store it in her Warehouse later, when it was safe to access it.

At the same time Count Li sent a mechanical bird flying back to the Soul Society. "I'll set some guards on this place," he told them. "I can't take anything unless Zhan Ping agrees, but at least we can protect it." A good idea, given the one behind this matter likely wasn't done yet.

弟子

Chang'an's Imperial City was several times larger than Khaitan's royal palace. Several times more elaborate, as well. Of course, it'd been built and rebuilt through several dynasties already. Likely the place had just kept growing, even when the current rulers weren't as powerful or influential as the last.

Qing's study of local history said there'd been a time when Chang'an had been the capitol of the much larger Sui kingdom. After Sui's fall, however, there'd been a good few hundred years of shifts between ruling families; Sui to Ling to Kang to the current An. And each new family had set their name on the kingdom, overwriting what'd been left behind.

Really, based on the size of An Kingdom, the Emperor's title was grandiose. There were other small kingdoms surrounding it and no one ruler commanding them all. Emperor An Ranshi might expand his influence someday but right now his kingdom was smaller than all of Khaitan.

If nothing else, the Emperor's servants did a good job of looking properly imperial. Their uniforms were all brocaded silk with designs that showed just how important they were by the sheer amount of embroidery covering them. They were beautiful and colorful but frankly, they looked awfully uncomfortable.

Qing and Xinglu were passed from servant to servant in successively more elaborate outfits, until—a full hour after they'd entered the city—they were met by a eunuch in red and gold, his softly rounded features belying his sharp and thoughtful gaze. "The Emperor will see you now," he said quietly.

Hadn't it been the Empress who'd called for him? Qing would have questioned the man but he turned and led them away without waiting for an answer. Realizing he'd get no explanations for the change, Qing followed, with Xinglu close behind.

They were led to a throne room, one filled with older men in formal robes. Xinglu leaned close. Whispered, "Government officials. Be on your best behavior."

Yearning to ask when he wasn't on his best behavior, Qing stayed meekly silent as they were led to the throne at the other end of the room. Following Xinglu's instructions, he knelt before the Emperor and kowtowed. "This Apprentice Qing of the Book Hunters Sect greets the Emperor," he said. "It is an honor."

Xinglu added, "This Apprentice Xinglu of the Soul Protection Society greets the Emperor. Offers apologies for any mistakes he might make."

"This Emperor bids Apprentice Qing and Apprentice Xinglu rise." The man's voice was momentarily familiar, though Qing couldn't say why. He obediently rose, looking up briefly to see a figure so covered in blue silk and gold and jewels that it impossible to tell what lay beneath. The man's face was partially hidden behind a half-mask of silk and feathers. His hands were concealed beneath glittering silken gloves.

"Apprentice Qing, this Emperor understands you to be a member of the Book Hunters, not a citizen of An Kingdom?"

"This Qing hails from Khaitan, as do all of our sect," Qing agreed, not sure if he was making trouble for himself or simply being honest. All too often it seemed like he managed both options simultaneously.

"We have heard of the Book Hunters. Heard too that you recently collected a scroll Our Wife gifted to our beloved Count Li."

Qing had almost forgotten about that annoying brat of a scroll. "This one and his Master did," he agreed.

"Word was the scroll was so full of magic it caused you trouble. Rumor has it that you even called in a dragon to help you."

Now they were to the point of discussing Qing himself, or rather, the dragon everyone seemed so determined to meet. "Respect, your Majesty, the dragon is fond of Master Zhi," Qing said truthfully. "And does what Master Zhi requires of him."

That made the Emperor fall silent, giving another speaker a chance to interrupt. "How interesting," the new voice said, drawing Qing's attention towards one of the Emperor's eunuch attendants. Not the one from earlier. This one was thin, pale, elderly; looking like a stiff wind would push him over. Yet his light voice held surprising strength.

"Eunuch Zhao, what is it you would say?" The Emperor sounded displeased.

"THIS EMPEROR BIDS APPRENTICE QING AND APPRENTICE XINGLI RISE."

If so, he didn't try to silence the man. Qing noted the name. The eunuch Kang Qiyun had warned him to watch out for.

"Her Imperial Majesty Ling Fei wishes for a chance to meet the dragon. Such an auspicious encounter might help ensure an heir. She sent me in hopes of requesting you permit it."

"Her Majesty, and you, overstep your bounds. The dragon is the symbol of the Emperor," an official snapped. "She'd no business calling for him, anyway!"

"The dragon isn't even here. There's no point asking for something that can't be found," yet another noted.

An argument began, only to be stopped by the Emperor saying softly, "Silence." A bit to Qing's surprise, it had the desired effect.

Once it was quiet, the Emperor said wearily, "This Emperor's Wife is overeager. Until the dragon descends among us, We're in no position to request its blessing on others." He turned his attention back to Qing. "Can you at least explain why the dragon failed to acknowledge Us?"

Qing really didn't understand why everyone was so excited about the idea. "Regret to correct you, Your Majesty. But the dragon in question is not an emissary of Heaven. Just a very young and inexperienced dragonling, barely transcended from carp. He cannot bring any message to or from the Gods, nor aid Her Majesty in providing an heir, if that's what's desired."

The Emperor fell silent and Qing could only hope he hadn't overstepped his bounds, saying things so bluntly. He fought the urge to clarify, to explain and excuse himself further. Fortunately, the Emperor finally said, "This Emperor was told the dragon was huge, a giant over a hundred feet long, all gold and silver."

As one of the Emperor's attendants coughed, sounding deeply embarrassed, Qing fought down incredulity. At his largest he was barely ten feet long and while his scales were silver and gold, they were also marked with blues and greens and purple, as befitted a Royal Blue Koi.

Knowing better than to laugh, Qing murmured, "He is much smaller than you describe and his scales have patches of other colors, much like the brocade carp some keep as pets." He hoped those markings were properly hidden by his robes.

A sigh of deep regret. "Then it was exaggeration and over-active imagination. Still, I don't suppose your Master can call her dragon to Us. If naught else, this Emperor would be fascinated to meet such a creature."

Qing bowed. "When the opportunity arises, this apprentice will gladly ask Master Zhi her opinion. At the moment, she's busy investigating the source of those fires and this apprentice should return to her."

The Emperor considered that. "Approach Me," he ordered suddenly, causing a stir of reaction throughout the room. Even Xinglu started, glancing sideways at Qing with a worried gaze.

Though Qing guessed it was almost unheard of for an outsider to be allowed near the Emperor, he silently stepped forwards and went to his knees at the base of the throne. "This Qing obeys," he murmured.

A dry, papery, hand grasped Qing's chin gently, tilting his face so they could look at each other. The man's features were hidden behind that half-mask of his, but he seemed surprisingly young and vaguely familiar. "You've worked hard. This Emperor grants you this gift." He slid a bracelet of black jade onto Qing's wrist, then released him. "Go now. Give my greetings to those you left behind. The two of you are dismissed."

Confused but knowing better than to show it, Qing rose and backed away from the throne. Immediately, the same eunuch who'd escorted them into court came to lead them out of the building, into the afternoon sunlight.

As they headed for the exit, a figure approached from the shadows of a nearby alley. Eunuch Zhao, his expression faintly mocking as he approached. "If the young apprentice is willing, Her Imperial Majesty still desperately desires a chance to speak with you."

Qing stared wide-eyed at the man, not at all sure how to say 'no'.

弟子

There being nothing aside from the hair stick that seemed useful, they roused Zhan Ping from her stupor and persuaded her to stand. "We'll have to discuss matters more carefully soon," Count Li told the woman. "But I want you in a better state of mind first."

Shen Wei's soothing powder left her just woozy and compliant enough to agree. Gods knew how she'd be once the stuff wore off but at least she was cooperative for the moment. The last thing they needed was another childish squabble for no reason whatsoever.

Zhan Ping was just barely awake enough to lock up her vault behind her and Zhi Wenku hoped she'd done a good job of it. That was another thing they didn't need; someone breaking in and getting at the woman's treasures. Nothing in there seemed dangerous but in some cases they were all Zhan Ping had left of her master and that made them important.

When they climbed the ladder they found young Li Aiqing waiting patiently outside, along with a dozen Soul Protection Society guards, all keeping an eye on things. The Count had meant it when he'd said he wanted the vault safe. Well enough, that'd keep looters from poking around until something could be done to repair the place.

"My brother wanted me to tell you, your apprentice was taken to meet the Empress," the boy said as they left the building.

What sort of nonsense was that? Zhi Wenku had heard the Empress was young and impetuous, but surely she knew better than to demand a young man be brought to her presence?

"Whatever for?"

A sigh. "Rumors of a dragon reached her. And dragons are supposed to be heavenly emissaries."

Oh for heaven's sake. "How is it no one can tell a baby dragon from an adult." It occurred to her that the only ones who should have known about Qing were those present. "And how did the Empress know about him, anyway?"

That set Li Aiqing flushing. "She doesn't know Apprentice Qing is a dragon. But everyone saw him flying around and Commander Fan came to find him. He insisted Qing go with him, since he said he knows the dragon."

Zhi Wenku sighed. So much unnecessary nonsense. "All right. I'll fetch him. I don't know what's going on but he's my apprentice and my responsibility."

"I'll come with you," Shen Wei said. "Xinglu must have gone along as support and he's my apprentice and my responsibility."

Turning her attention on Count Li and Pang Hua, Zhi Wenku indicated the woman the pair supported between them. "She's had a difficult day. I suggest you get her to a doctor and let her rest before we continue this. As soon as we've got Qing and Xinglu we'll come back to discuss the situation."

Both men agreed and Pang Hua lifted Zhan Ping in his arms. "I'll take her back and wait for you, then." Without waiting for acknowledgement, he headed off, leaving Count Li to add, "You'll need my help getting into the Imperial City. Shen Wei won't be enough, given who's involved."

That was true enough and Zhi Wenku followed the man through Chang'an to one of the smaller wooden doors at the side of the wall surrounding the Imperial City. Bypassing the guards, Count Li led the way through the maze of streets to the main road.

Two familiar figures headed towards them, causing Zhi Wenku to sigh with relief. "They're safe."

"Did you think they weren't?"

"There was no guarantee that boy of mine kept his true nature secret," Zhi Wenku told Shen Wei, putting the image of a carp with its mouth wide, wide, wide open on her fan. "And no guarantee the Empress wanted to meet a dragon because she thinks they're delightful. Dragonlings like Qing are a prime source of magical materials, you realize."

"My dear, I am an alchemist, unless you've forgotten."

Count Li interrupted. "Best act quickly." He pointed at a man in court robes approaching from a nearby walkway, a half-dozen guards behind him. "That's Eunuch Zhao and his personal guard. The Emperor and Empress aren't threats, but I wouldn't lay any bets on him."

As Eunuch Zhao spoke to the pair, causing Qing's eyes to go wide with confusion and worry, Zhi Wenku stepped forward and interrupted calmly, "There you are, boy. Come along. There's work to be done and I've no time for nonsense."

Ignoring Eunuch Zhao, she walked forward, Shen Wei and Count Li close behind her.

弟子

Relief flooded Qing at the sight of his master. He would have run straight to her, forgetting manners and sense, if not for her warning gaze. Her fan flipped up briefly with the word, [[Wait]] on its surface. By the time Eunuch Zhao looked, the word was gone.

"Uninvited outsiders in the Imperial City?" the eunuch demanded, glaring coldly at Count Li as he joined them. "Did you bring these two in here?"

Count Li gave the man the briefest of acknowledgments. Turned to look at the eunuch leading Qing and Xinglu. "They've seen the Emperor already, Eunuch Kang?"

"They have, Count Li. I was just escorting them out when Eunuch Zhao insisted on speaking with them. He says Empress Ling Fei wants to meet them."

There'd been faint threat beneath Eunuch Zhao's request. A sense Qing wouldn't be allowed to refuse. The half dozen guards hiding in the shadows of the alley nearby made that much clear. Sure his elders knew about those men, Qing just said, "I was about to tell him I needed your permission, Master Zhi."

"Given." Master Zhi's answer startled Qing, though he didn't show it and just waited for her to continue, "As long as Master Shen and I accompany them. The boys are still quite young. They don't know what should and should not be said."

That wasn't true at all—one of the many things Master Zhi had taught Qing was how to behave in front of royalty—but Qing didn't protest. It was obvious why his Master denigrated his good sense. Equally obvious why she wanted involved.

A dour look. "This Eunuch would gladly invite all of you to the Empress's court, but fears he cannot." He spread his hands in a helpless gesture. "It was one thing to bring invited guests. Quite another to exhaust her with two extra people. Perhaps Master Zhi and Master Shen would allow their apprentices to visit alone?"

Qing deliberately looked foolish, gazing with wide-eyed wonder at his Master, as if he actually wanted to meet Empress Ling Fei. It was part of an act he and Master Zhi often played. Her, the long-suffering guardian putting up with his nonsense. Him, the poor easily cheated fool, if only the cheater could get him alone and unprotected.

Unfortunately for Eunuch Zhao, there was no way Master Zhi would permit Qing to wander around the Imperial City. She'd long since warned him that royal courts were hotbeds of intrigue and conspiracy. Innocent young koi, no matter how far transcended to dragon-hood, had no business playing such games.

Giving Eunuch Zhao a long look, Master Zhi finally said, "Apprentice Qing and Apprentice Xinglu are both young and enthusiastic. Without the two of us along to keep them in check, I fear they would be far too much of a handful. If Empress Ling Fei is in poor health it'd be cruel to force her to endure their uncontrolled antics."

Master Shen added, "Perhaps another time, Eunuch Zhao. Master Zhi and her apprentice are staying at the Soul Protection Society as guests. If Her Imperial Majesty feels she is up to the four of us visiting, or even just Master Zhi and Apprentice Qing, you can send word."

For a brief moment Qing feared the eunuch would call his guards in to help. Eunuch Zhao's lips tightened on his anger, though, and he cupped his hands, bowing politely. "This Zhao will bring word to the Empress and prepare for a better time and place," he agreed, finally returning the way he'd come. His guards left as well, leaving the six of them standing in the middle of the empty street.

Master Shen turned to Xinglu. Examined him carefully, fan waving with a thoughtful air as the man made sure his apprentice had taken no hurt during his tribulation. "It seems you've done well."

"I have, sir!" Xinglu grinned brightly, adding, "I should be able to hold my beast form better now, without risking losing control. And you have to see my weapons exercise!" He reached into his sleeve, clearly going to pull out the big saber he'd had to hide away during their visit to the Emperor.

A sharp rap from Master Shen's fan stopped the boy. "Hey! Ow!"

"We're still in the middle of the Imperial City, child. Is this the place to be drawing blades and showing off your cultivation?"

"Oh. Uhm. No."

Qing grinned. To be fair, he'd nearly done the same sort of thing when he'd first become a dragonling, so he understood just how Xinglu felt. "We can test it out later," he told his friend. "For now we really need to get back to Soul Protection Society. If Eunuch Kang would be willing to lead us?"

Eunuch Kang, who'd been watching with a quietly cynical expression, agreed, gesturing ahead of them. "I've nothing pressing to interfere at the moment, so I'll lead you back outside." He glanced around, clearly aware they were being watched, and added, "The sooner you're gone, the better."

Now that was a truth Qing wouldn't argue with.

CHAPTER 7
The Secret of the Scroll

By the time they'd returned to the Soul Protection Society's headquarters, Zhi Wenku had told Qing and Xinglu what they'd found in Zhan Ping's vault. Qing and Xinglu also managed a fairly succinct explanation of their meeting with the Emperor. Succinct and at the same time, somehow incomprehensible.

"It doesn't make sense," she muttered as the central platform inside Count Li's tower carried them to the upper floors. "What was that all about?"

Shen Wei told her, "You've already noticed how revered dragons are in this land. There are monstrous dragons, of course, the kind no one wants anywhere near them. But small and young though Qing is, he's still quite impressive to those who never see his kind. Whereas you, a native of Khaitan and his Master, can't help but see him as a child."

For a moment that didn't make sense. Then Zhi Wenku rethought it and understood. "I think I see your point," she admitted. "But this is annoying. Why did you have to go and transcend to dragonling state, Qing? You weren't so noticeable as a dragon-carp."

That was ignored as it deserved to be. Instead Qing said, "What I don't understand is why the Emperor gave me this bracelet." He tapped the black circlet around his wrist, drawing Zhi Wenku's sharp attention. "Is something wrong, Master?"

"Haven't I taught you not to just take gifts and use them?" Zhi Wenku demanded. "Remove it at once."

He did so, holding the glossy piece of jewelry on his palm with an uncomfortable expression. "I'm sorry, Master. I didn't think."

Trying not to panic, reminding herself that her apprentice was clearly safe and unharmed, Zhi Wenku took the bracelet and examined it. "At the very least you should have checked it for *qi*," she scolded, doing so herself. Nothing. All it was, was a solid piece of black jade, unmarked and unremarkable.

She corrected herself. Not solid. Not unmarked. Not as unremarkable as she'd first thought. This was a mechanist device, a torus of almost perfectly smooth black jade, with a series of five faint circles marking the outermost edge. Five rotating rings were embedded around the torus, each marked with the twelve animals of the local zodiac.

The platform halted at the top of the tower and the gate opened to let them step out. "I think this is involved with that hair stick."

"That makes no sense," Count Li protested, leading the way back to his sitting room. "Why would the Emperor have any of Master Pan Wei's things? May I see it?"

Zhi Wenku handed the bracelet over. "Is it familiar?"

Count Li frowned. "Pan Wei had a bracelet he always wore, yes, but it was wrapped in silk. Why do you think it has anything to do with that hair stick?"

After a moment to organize her thoughts and make sure she was clear, Zhi Wenku told him, "You recall what I said was written on the inside of that hair stick's prongs? Elements on one, five zodiacal beasts on the other."

"I do."

Zhi Wenku went to the Count's desk and gestured at the writing implements, "May I?" At his agreement, she drew the bracelet, marking the location of the five rotating rings. "These parts each have the twelve animals of your zodiac carved onto them. The rings turn, so that you could put any combination of five animals up on one side of the bracelet."

"That would be an impressive number of combinations," Shen Wei murmured. "Not impossible to force if you didn't know it, but damned hard." He took the bracelet from Count Li without bothering to ask, ignoring his Chief Cultivator's raised brow in favor of fiddling with the rings. "Let's see. If memory serves me right, my dear, you said 'rooster, snake, tiger, rat, goat'?"

If Zhi Wenku had found any *qi* at all in the bracelet she would have stopped Shen Wei. The thing was a mechanism, though, and too small to contain anything truly dangerous. Or at least she hoped so. "I did and I'm impressed you remember all that."

"Some pills get feisty if you take too long making them. I have to remember things without pausing to check the recipe," Shen Wei pointed out as he turned his attention on the bracelet. "The one trouble is not knowing which ring is first. I'll have to try all five combinations."

He did so and sighed in disappointment when nothing happened. "This could take a while."

Xinglu offered. "Each ring might correspond to one of the elements. Maybe you have to take that into account as well?"

"Good thinking," Shen Wei told his apprentice. He turned and turned the wheels, repeating the task until he'd tried every combination. At last he sighed. "Not constructive order. Destructive?" He tried again. "No. Still nothing. Should I try starting with a different element first?"

A chuckle from Count Li. "Perhaps.... But Master Shen, you're forgetting what was written on the other prong of the hair stick."

It took Zhi Wenku a moment to remember herself. "The elements." She paused, visualizing the words and added, "Earth, metal, wood, water, fire... That's not right."

"I remembered thinking two elements—wood and water—were out of order," Count Li agreed. "But that's more than enough. Try switching tiger and rat, Master Shen."

Again Shen Wei turned and turned the rings, until—on the third try—something clicked and the faint circles Zhi Wenku had noticed around the outer edge of the bracelet became cylinders poking outwards at varying lengths.

"It looks just like a key's wards," Xinglu said, fascinated.

Giving him an approving look, Shen Wei told him, "Well noted, Xinglu. I suspect it, and the hair stick, are keys to something important."

"But what?"

"Almost certainly Pan Wei's craft hall," Count Li said as Shen Wei handed the bracelet to Zhi Wenku. "As I mentioned earlier, it wasn't destroyed, being well protected inside the mountain. But no one's been able to get past the doors since he died."

"Then this may be the key. And whoever is behind those fires might be trying to get their hands on it." Zhi Wenku reached into her *qiankun* sleeve and pulled out her Warehouse, intending to put the hair stick and bracelet away. "I'll keep them both safely hidden," she began, opening her Warehouse.

Except as she did so, something rushed out the opening, slamming into her and knocking her to the floor. She shook herself, a bit too startled to take in what'd just happened. Things in her Warehouse were supposed to behave. They didn't come flying out without her intending them to.

Zhi Wenku looked around to see Count Li setting a shield array on the windows, Shen Wei blocking the door and Qing and Xinglu reenacting, almost perfectly, the scene in Count Li's mansion just a day or so earlier. Up to and including chasing that damned annoying brat of a scroll.

弟子

The last time Qing chased the scroll, he'd had to turn dragon and follow it into the sky. This time Count Li's quick reactions, together with Master Shen's, meant the thing had nowhere to go. Not that that stopped it from trying.

Qing pulled a capture cloth from his *qiankun* sleeve. He didn't like to use this tool because it risked damaging fragile pages, but he didn't think that was a problem here. Not when the scroll kept slamming into walls and shelves and people. As wildly and uncontrollably as it rushed around, the scroll should have been ripped and torn to pieces within a minute.

Xinglu leapt for the scroll, still human in form but trying to chomp down on it as if he were a dog and his target a rather large and unwieldy stick. Meanwhile, Master Zhi moved slowly, shifting her position so she could drive the scroll towards Qing.

Oddly enough, the combination of Master Zhi's calm stalking and Xinglu's wild yelps and leaps proved effective. Xinglu couldn't move as fast as the scroll but he kept its attention by flinging himself around, giving Master Zhi a chance to slowly corner it, with Qing preparing to throw his cloth over the thing.

Ordinarily, that would have done the job. Instead, forced against the wall, the scroll opened briefly, flinging a dozen paper and metal rabbits into their faces. Master Zhi knocked the creatures away with her whisk, but that gave the scroll a chance to fly past her, heading for the door, a larger and heavier rabbit leaping towards Master Shen.

To his credit, Master Shen held his ground, using his fan to force the rabbit back while he grabbed for the scroll. He hit the first but missed the latter, as it rushed towards the window and Count Li's array. That proved its downfall. The array folded around it, fine lines of purple-tinted light forming the shape of an inverted umbrella, closing around its captive tightly.

"Give that annoying little brat here. I'm going to lock it in the cold chamber until it learns its lesson," Master Zhi snapped as Count Li reached into his array to pull the scroll out. "Gods know what sort of mess it's made in my Warehouse."

"A moment, Master Zhi. I have a theory." Count Li grasped the scroll tightly, trying to unroll it, despite its obvious resistance. He won the fight after several moments of tugging and pulling.

Spread open, the scroll appeared blank, though Qing would have sworn it hadn't been before. They'd not had time to examine it, being too busy with the situation in Chang'an, but he'd opened it back when he'd caught it earlier, long enough to see the title and author: The Artifice of Design, by Dai Qingfu.

When Qing told them that, Zhi Wenku frowned. "Dai Qingfu? That doesn't sound like a real name."

"I'm certain it isn't." Count Li shook the scroll hard, adding, "Unless I'm mistaken, the Qingfu means frivolous, doesn't it, Apprentice Qing?"

It did. "Why does that matter?" Writers often took odd names when they published their work.

"It matters because it's a perfect description of a certain incredibly brilliant and incredibly foolish artificer and mechanist of my acquaintance. One I thought long dead, killed by his own apprentice's machinations." Count Li tapped the scroll hard. "Pan Wei, enough games. Come out of there this minute."

There was silence, mostly because they were all staring at the scroll, half expecting someone to step right out of it the way Count Li suggested. Instead a featureless little doll of wire and paper dropped to the floor between them. It jumped onto the largest rabbit's back and rode around the room briefly, then clambered up onto the Count's desk so it could use his brushes.

As the other paper rabbits scampered back into the scroll, the doll wrote on a blank sheet, [[Oh, hey, hi there, Old Li. I didn't realize it was you. Hard to tell what's going on outside. Was afraid it was that dragon again, going to eat me this time.]]

Now that wasn't fair at all. "I was not going to eat you."

That drew the doll's attention to Qing. [[I said a dragon was going to eat... oh, wait... are you the dragon? Now I really am embarrassed. Uhm... Sorry? I didn't realize you were sentient.]]

While Qing tried to think what sort of dragon wasn't sentient, Master Zhi demanded, "You really are Pan Wei?"

[[This is just a doll and Pan Wei's body died about a hundred and thirty years ago.]]

Count Li tapped the doll—lightly—atop its head. "Don't play word games, Pan Wei."

[[Hah! No. True. There isn't time. At least, I don't think there's time? I'm not sure. I lost a bit of myself, saving myself. Broke my *hun* soul into three parts and I think one died."

Hun souls were said to have three separate aspects; life, intellect and emotion. "Where's the third?" Zhi Wenku asked.

[[My memory's really bad, but I think it's in my craft hall. Can you maybe get me inside?]]

Count Li murmured, "I'm not sure that's a good idea, Pan Wei. We seem to have someone trying to gain access, and we think they're willing to burn Chang'an to the ground to get at your key."

[[Burn Chang'an?]] The puppet jounced around as it thought about that. Then, [[I can't see or hear much through the scroll. You have to be talking right in front of it while it's open. So I don't know what's going on. Could you, please, please, pretty please, tell me?]]

With a sigh, Count Li settled into a chair and set to doing just that.

弟子

It took Count Li several minutes to go over the last few days' events. By the time he was done, Zhi Wenku felt sorry for Pan Wei. His paper doll sat on the edge of the desk looking terribly dejected, especially when the Count mentioned their theory that the Pot of Ten Thousand Crows was Daoping's copy. "Unless you had Zhan Ping make one too, that is."

The paper doll sat silent for a moment, clearly trying to remember. Then it popped up on its small feet and wrote, [[I didn't. Da Ping was better at mechanisms. Pingping was her father's daughter and she wanted to make him happy, so she focused on artifice.]]

Zhi Wenku reflected that there was something terribly childish about Pan Wei's way of naming people. That and it must have been confusing, having two apprentices with such similar names.

[[Oh. Ohohohohoh!]] Ink slopped around the page in Pan Wei's excitement. [[I wonder... was that why that *jiangshi* attacked Shishi? Was it trying to get at the forbidden treasures?]]

Replacing the paper with a fresh page, Count Li asked, "Who's Shishi? And what *jiangshi*?"

Zhi Wenku had a bad feeling she knew. Nor was she surprised when Pan Wei wrote, [[Oh, yes. Sorry. Lord High Emperor An Ranshi.]] The puppet looked like it was giggling as it wrote, showing just how seriously Pan Wei didn't take the Emperor or his titles. [[Feifei begged me to make a new arm for him. Don't tell him. He doesn't know.]]

Ignoring the childishness, Zhi Wenku asked, "A new arm?"

[[Yeah. Feifei... I mean Her Royal Majesty, Empress Ling Fei... asked me to help him. My scroll's been with her family for generations and we've been friends since she was little and you're asking why he needed an arm, aren't you?]]

Zhi Wenku just waited, watching the doll silently, waiting for it to finish its story. In an embarrassed fashion it continued, [[Feifei told me someone broke into the forbidden treasures vault in his study. When he went to investigate the noise, something like a *jiangshi* attacked him.]]

Qing had mentioned the Emperor's hand feeling like paper and metal. Apparently artificers and mechanists had preferred working materials. Zhi Wenku set that thought aside for later as Count Li asked warily, "Forbidden treasures?"

[[Yep. Shishi found a cache of the things in the vault under his office after he was crowned. Feifei told me he thought they'd been there ever since his ancestor, An Lixing, took power. He didn't dare touch them or mention them, for fear they'd get used. Guess that didn't work out for him.]]

That didn't make Count Li happy at all. Nor should it, based on some of the things Daoping created. "I should have guessed," Count Li grumbled. "I brought them all together to destroy, but someone must have snuck some of them out somehow. Humanity is just so clever when it comes to cutting their own feet off for the sake of greed."

Zhi Wenku considered that. "Were any of the items in Zhan Ping's vault part of Daoping's work?"

"None that I recognized. It isn't impossible, of course, but I honestly don't think she'd have wanted to keep any of it."

Unless Zhan Ping was especially good at dissembling, that seemed unlikely. Zhi Wenku thought about it, visualizing the list of items in the vault, keeping in mind her theory that different artificers and mechanists preferred different materials. Then, "There's an umbrella in Zhan Ping's vault," she said. "Its materials were different from your preferences. Parchment—which is made of hide—and wood, not paper and metal. Was it your work, Master Pan?"

[[Not if it's parchment and wood. Sounds like the one Pingping made. It didn't work, though, not even as a proper umbrella. I never did find time to work out why.]]

Count Li tilted his head at Pan Wei's paper doll. "You truly had her attempt a copy of the World Umbrella? That seems singularly unwise. Did she try again?"

[[No idea. She was more interested in the Five Color Brush, anyway.]]

That was what led to the woman's turning on her master and usurping her brother's throne. Zhi Wenku might have pointed that out but she'd a more important question. "Working or not, how did Zhan Ping acquire that umbrella? I can't see her keeping something Daoping made out of sentimentality."

[[I don't know. I had it in my craft hall, last I remember. But that was a long time ago.]]

Shen Wei asked, "Is it possible our unknown enemy wanted the umbrella?"

They thought about that, though poor Qing was way over his head, big dark eyes wide with confusion. Zhi Wenku didn't blame him. The situation was convoluted and he was a koi of most direct thoughts, a point he immediately proved by asking, "I thought it was the hair stick? Wouldn't that be more important?"

Excitedly, Pan Wei's paper doll wrote, [[Hair stick? You have my hair stick? That's good, very good! You can get me into my craft hall... oh, wait, you need my bracelet, too. Better ask Feifei for that. I gave it to her.]]

Well, that confirmed their theory regarding both pieces, though not how the Emperor had gotten hold of the latter. "We have it already," Zhi Wenku told him. "But I don't think we should go to your craft hall now."

The paper doll wilted. [[Oh. But why not? I could help you better if I could think more clearly. I told you my memory's all messed up, thanks to breaking my *hun* soul up. I did tell you that, right?]]

He was proving his point. From what Zhi Wenku understood, breaking apart one's *hun* soul could damage it badly. "Your craft hall contains all your work, right? If the enemy wants access, do you think it's a good idea to open it up?"

"It'd be a terrible mistake," Count Li said firmly. "So far all they've managed has been two relatively small fires."

"I don't think the people who lost family and homes and belongings agree that they were small fires," Shen Wei pointed out. "You tend to forget things like that."

Count Li smiled wistfully. "I do, I admit it. Yes. Those fires were quite bad for those affected. Letting the enemy get ahold of anything stronger would be far worse."

Seeing the mood shift, Qing did what Qing did best and asked another innocent question, "Shouldn't we ask Master Zhan about the umbrella?"

[Da Ping is here? I'd love to talk to her!] Pan Wei agreed readily, gesturing for the Count to hold his scroll open again and leaping back inside. Now his chaotic writing showed on the surface of the scroll. [[This is easier than having you carry ink and paper around.]]

"It is," Count Li agreed. "Can you hear me?"

[[I only hear a little with the scroll closed. You'll have to open it and talk directly in my... ah... face if you want me to understand.]]

They left the Count's meeting room, heading for the Society's guest quarters, only to be stopped part of the way by Senior Yao. The man looked absolutely flustered and infuriated. "Chief Cultivator Li. You have got to do something about that woman and those young fools you adopted!"

"I do?" Amusement suffused Count Li's face, as if he could already guess at the situation. "Whatever for?"

"That woman is telling my apprentices and me my business. And Li Aiqing played with my bird calling device and now we have a hundred hungry pigeons flying around inside. And that Pang Hua fellow is doing nothing to stop any of this!"

"All of which seems perfectly in character," the Count murmured. "Shen Wei, whatever did you give her, anyway? Is she intoxicated?"

"She shouldn't be. It was just a soporific, sir."

They hurried through the building to another, this one covered in protective sigils and surrounded by a guardian array. As Zhi Wenku wondered if any of the Soul Protection Society's development halls were actually safe, Count Li led the way into a large room with several dozen craft tables and a number of confused but fascinated apprentices and disciples.

The two young guards—who Zhi Wenku suspected made it their goal in life to make the worst possible choices—rushed back and forth, trying to shoo thousands of pigeons out an open window. It was a fruitless attempt because the ceiling was a good fifteen feet high and neither could jump more than five feet. An impressive height, really, but useless when one was trying to chase creatures who could fly beyond their reach.

As Senior Yao had said, Pang Hua wasn't helping at all. He leaned lazily against a table, watching the fuss and occasionally offering unhelpful advice. "Maybe if you squirted them."

"I think they tried that already," Captain Li pointed out from his position near the door.

"We did! Remember?"

"They don't even notice and now the room stinks of wet pigeon!"

"Try squirting them with perfume," Pang Hua countered.

Fortunately, for all their talent at choosing bad ideas, the youngsters didn't try that plan. They weren't succeeding, but at least they weren't making things stink to the Emperor of Heaven's throne in the process.

Zhi Wenku turned her attention on Zhan Ping, who'd gathered the apprentices together to discuss their work. "Now this is good," she was saying, examining one student's diagram. "Simple. Elegant. Have you chosen your preferred materials yet? You'll need two to start, you understand?"

"Teacher Yao wants us to try working with one material only," one youngster said.

"Oh, that's foolish," Zhan Ping began and Senior Yao growled a curse from behind Zhi Wenku. Ignoring the noise, Zhan Ping went on, "Even if you're just beginning you want one solid and one malleable. No gas or liquids, though. That's high level stuff, especially air. The only one I know could use it has been dead for over a century."

Count Li sighed. "This could go on for hours if I know this lot. We don't have time." He turned pleading eyes on Zhi Wenku. "Could your apprentice help with those birds?"

弟子

Zhi Wenku gestured at Qing, who happily ran to help chase the pigeons out of the hall, close followed by Xinglu. As Count Li went to get Zhan Ping's attention, Zhi Wenku reflected that she'd have to find time to discuss how artificers worked in more depth. Later, when their other problem was dealt with.

"TRY SQUIRTING THEM WITH PERFUME."

Unlike Kang Qiyun and Li Aiqing, Qing knew he could easily handle the pigeons. Except he was interrupted just as he was getting ready to shapeshift to his dragon form. Senior Yao, who apparently had firm opinions of what was right and proper, caught his arm. "Don't you even dare turn into a dragon in here, young man."

"Sir, I promise...."

"You're far too big for this room. You'll break something, flying around inside."

For one thing, Qing could be anything between palm-sized to something approximating several elephants. For another, the room was huge, with more than enough space for him to fly around. For a third, dragons didn't fly the way most creatures flew.

Still, he didn't want to argue and he did have another way to fly. He pulled his whisk from his sleeve and used it to float in mid-air. Behind him, Xinglu drew his sword and did the same, so that within moments the pair of them were zooming around above Kang Qiyun and Li Aiqing, forcing the pigeons to keep flying.

Senior Yao made noises like a cat ready to cough up a hairball. Not that Qing blamed him, since the birds contained a truly amazing quantity of droppings, all of which they frantically released. Nor did they come close to cooperating with their pursuit, trying to fly past the two of them whenever they had a chance. Oh, but Qing had an idea. He pulled out his capture cloth and tossed one end to Xinglu. "Hey, catch!"

"Do we actually want to keep these feathered rats?" Xinglu asked, grasping his end of the cloth tightly. "I mean, they're not even tasty. Have you seen what city pigeons eat?"

Qing hadn't even considered that. "We just want to encourage them to leave. Chase them out the window."

They did so easily now, to the great amusement of both Pang Hua and the students. Senior Yao was still making that sick cat noise of his but at least they got the birds out. The mess they'd left behind, however, would be someone else's problem.

Landing, putting away his whisk and going to join Master Zhi and the others, Qing grinned at the image of fireworks forming on his master's fan. Master Shen's displayed constantly blooming flowers, which Qing guessed was his way of approving Xinglu's work. At least Xinglu's expression said that was what it meant.

"That was fantastic," Kang Qiyun exclaimed as Xinglu and Qing landed. "Really great! Being a dragon has to be incredible!"

That made Master Zhi sigh. "What did I say about not idolizing him?" As the young man flushed with embarrassment, she turned to Captain Li. "Why in the world are you here? And why bring these two nuisances?"

As both Li Aiqing and Kang Qiyun protested, Captain Li spread his hands. "The Emperor wants to know the situation. He trusts me to help him find out."

Unconvinced but clearly unwilling to pursue the point, Master Zhi went over to where Count Li was talking with Master Zhan. He wasn't having much success, because the woman looked ready to lose her temper, much as she apparently had back in her vault.

Master Zhi had told Qing they thought the Five Color Brush affected her thinking, making it difficult for her to accept certain truths. "I have no idea what umbrella you're talking about," she growled at Count Li, sounding like Xinglu when faced with something bigger and stronger than himself.

"You were with us in your vault, Master Zhan," Count Li said gently. "Do you not recall the umbrella we found? It's even in your record book. Pan Wei's notes said it didn't even keep off rain."

"What about it? It's not important."

"Did you make it?" Master Zhi asked, though they were all sure she hadn't. "Or Daoping?"

The woman frowned fiercely. "If it was in my vault it's either mine or what little I rescued from Master Pan's craft hall."

Qing had a feeling Master Zhan was losing her self control again. He glanced at Count Li with wide eyes and pointed at the scroll in his hands. Maybe it'd help if Master Pan could talk to her? To his relief, Count Li smiled approvingly, opening the scroll and turning its seemingly blank surface towards Master Zhan.

"I have no idea what you intend, Chief Cultivator, but...."

"Master Zhan, could I trouble you to look at this?" Count Li tapped the scroll, adding more loudly, "She's your student. You talk to her."

Before Master Zhan could react, either with bafflement or anger, the scroll formed the words, [[Hey there, Da Ping. Been a while. You doing okay?]]

Silence. Shocked, empty, silence. Master Zhan's expression went from coldly angry to bewildered and wistful and full of desperation. "That... that looks like... Master Pan's... handwriting."

[[Not looks like. Is.]] A drawing of a young man's face formed on the page, then the words, [[Ah, sorry about this.]]

"I don't understand. I don't understand. I really don't understand."

Qing could hardly blame the lady. "He put his soul into the scroll. Part of his soul, that is," he explained, though he probably should have his elders talk. They didn't stop him, perhaps counting on his youth and naïveté to soften Master Zhan's anger. Encouraged, Qing added helpfully, "With his version of the Five Color Brush."

[[A much better version than Pingping's, really,]] Pan Wei added.

"That's not possible. You told me your brush wasn't strong enough to create a place for a whole person."

"He split himself," Qing explained.

[[The child's right, Da Ping. I barely got it done before Pingping sent her men to capture me. Good thing I locked up my craft hall. They would have done it a mischief, otherwise.]]

That was a mistake on Pan Wei's part, because Master Zhan went white and red and—just as she had in the vault—lost her temper. "YOUR CRAFT HALL WAS DESTROYED!"

Before Pan Wei could dig deeper and make things worse, Master Zhi set a hand on Master Zhan's shoulder. "My dear, we aren't here to argue that point. If it's gone, it's gone. Let's concern ourselves with the question of that umbrella. You do recall its presence in your vault?"

Master Zhan calmed down. Said quietly, "I remember it being there. I don't remember who made it." She frowned. "Did... did Daoping use the brush to make me forget that?"

The fact that she was able to think clearly enough to work that out said it might be possible to undo the brush's effects, or at least work around them. Qing tilted his head, asking, "Master Pan, didn't you say you had a secret workshop? One further away from Chang'an, so it'd be safer? Maybe it came from there?"

Master Zhi eyed Qing approvingly. The others gave him equally approving looks and Qing wondered if he was blushing as heavily as he thought. Surely his face was bright red at this point.

If it was, no one said so. Master Pan's scroll went silent for several seconds, then, [[My craft... Oh, of course, my secret workshop. Yes. Da Ping, you know where it is. Up on Fenghua Shan? Not far from where my craft hall used to be... before it was... ah... burned?]]

For a moment Qing wasn't sure the trick would work. Master Zhan's expression shifted back and forth between rage to confusion to hope. Then, "Oh. Yes, that's right. I remember that place. You had me lock it up tight when you realized what Daoping was doing. I did, too. Though I don't know where the combination lock is. All I had was the key, and you know it resets every time."

[[Don't worry about that. We shouldn't try to get in yet. Now, about that umbrella. Did you maybe grab it from my craft... I mean from my workshop when you locked it up?]]

"I don't think so. I don't even remember where I got it." The woman frowned. "Why is the umbrella even important?"

"A good question," Count Li murmured. "But the fact that you're having trouble remembering how you acquired it says it might be important. I think we need to examine it more carefully."

Without needing to be ordered to fetch the thing, with a grin and a salute, Pang Hua leapt out the window into the late afternoon shadows.

弟子

Having sent Pang Hua to fetch the umbrella, the Count led them back towards his tower. "I feel we're missing something," he said. "We might want to.... Yes?"

The last was spoken to the small servant who'd come running boldly up to them as they walked. She held out a card with fine and elegant writing on it. Zhi Wenku caught the words "Flowery Delight" on its surface before Count Li put it away.

"I see, child. Run along and say, 'of course'." Once the girl was gone, Count Li turned to them, adding, "We've been invited to meet someone who could shed some light on matters."

Zhan Ping stopped. "I've had a difficult day and all I want is rest."

"Mm. A good point." Count Li called another servant over. "Escort Master Zhan to the guest quarters, would you? Make sure she's fully accommodated."

"I've no need...."

"You do, though. Your house may not be afire anymore, but I'm sure it stinks of smoke and lamp oil. Our guest house is safe for you and your master." He gestured at the scroll in her arms.

The reminder persuaded Zhan Ping to accept Soul Protection Society's hospitality and she went off, not happily but at least not complaining.

Soon after, they left the Soul Protection Society and headed for the center of town. As they walked, Zhi Wenku realized they were still accompanied by Captain Li and his two companions. She raised a brow at them, eliciting a slight shrug from Captain Li. "The Emperor was curious about the situation," he said. "He also wanted me to tell you about that scroll of Pan Wei's."

There were times when it was better to listen to what wasn't said and she'd a feeling this was one of them. The Emperor was definitely involved in this mess. The question was, how? "You know what the scroll contains?"

"A bloody nuisance, that's what," Kang Qiyun muttered. A moment later he exclaimed painfully, as Captain Li's knuckle tapped the young man on the back of his thick skull. "What was that for?"

"You talk too much. Be silent."

A sigh, followed by Count Li's chuckle as he admitted, "I adopted you and your brother to keep me grounded," he told the Captain. "I didn't realize it'd be so entertaining, as well."

"Mm. One strives to be of use." Captain Li turned his attention back to Zhi Wenku. "We grew up at the Emperor's side. He trusts us with things he wouldn't, or at least shouldn't, trust with anyone else."

So it'd seemed. "How did he get the scroll and why did it end up in Count Li's mansion?"

A sour look from Kang Qiyun. "The scroll belongs to the Empress and it was she who sent it. Without bothering to mention what she was doing, I might add."

"Why not?"

Now Kang Qiyun truly looked disgusted. "Because, and I quote, 'The Emperor was too busy malingering to talk to her.' Honestly. That magic arm she got for him doesn't make recovering any easier. Having your arm ripped off hurts!"

That was right. Pan Wei had mentioned the *jiangshi* that'd attacked the Emperor, forcing Pan Wei to build him a replacement arm. "Perhaps it would have been wiser to send it to the Soul Protection Society instead?"

"She's just a baby. She doesn't know better... HEY, stop flicking my head!"

Count Li chuckled as Kang Qiyun glared at his Captain, suggesting, "It's possible she was concerned that Eunuch Zhao would interfere. If I remember correctly, he watches her doings closely."

That did make some sense. Palace intrigue was something Zhi Wenku mostly avoided, but she did know how troublesome it could be. She would have said as much, but by this time they'd arrived at a large two story wooden building with huge pillars along the front and a sign reading "House of Flowery Delight". Men and women entered through the main doors, but Zhi Wenku's sharp eyes noted a second, more discreet entrance off to the side.

"This is a brothel?"

Shen Wei's fan showed delicate flowers fluttering in a breeze. At the same time he said, "The main building is a proper restaurant. Excellent and quite expensive. I'm not sure we're properly dressed for such a place."

"Mm. Don't worry. You're my guests. No one will say a word." Count Li handed the card from earlier to the servant who came to greet them. "We've been invited."

The servant didn't so much as blink. "Of course. Right this way, sirs. Madam." He led them through elegantly decorated halls to a large room, its walls covered in fine silk, a low table at the center with glass bottles of wine, a pot of tea and dozens of fiddly little snacks. Someone played a pipa in the room next door, their silhouette cast against silken hangings. Whoever it was, they were small and delicate. They were also quite good.

Zhi Wenku glanced curiously at the musician's shadow and noted the Count's complete lack of concern for the woman's presence. Expected, then? "A lovely setting," she murmured. "Albeit somewhat suspicious, given the circumstances."

"An understandable concern, although I assure you, quite unnecessary." A new voice spoke from the room beyond, and a slender, soft-faced man entered the room. Eunuch Kang, the one who'd been leading Qing and Xinglu out of the Imperial City.

"Then you invited us, sir?" Zhi Wenku asked, not wishing to waste time.

"On behalf of my mistress." Eunuch Kang indicated the shadow on the curtain, adding, "She would meet you and your apprentice incognito, Master Zhi, in hopes that you will be willing to help her and her husband."

Zhi Wenku contemplated the possibilities. A eunuch of the Imperial Palace might call a superior official 'master' but there were no female officials in An Kingdom's government. The only women who'd qualify for the title would be the wives and daughters of the Emperor. Moreover, the current Emperor had no children, only one wife and no consorts. By that logic, there really was only one person the woman on the other side of that curtain could be. Only one person who'd expressed a desire to meet Qing in his dragon form and hoped for his aid.

The question was, why was the Empress playing this intriguing charade?

弟子

Qing turned a worried look on his master, spotting the telltale signs of impatience with political games. Master Zhi didn't care for such things, even among her fellow Book Hunters. Qing's being dragged off to the palace earlier had irritated her, even if it had resulted in him being given the combination lock to Master Pan's craft hall.

Master Zhi took a calming breath, restoring herself. "I don't speak to people who refuse to face me."

That made Captain Li and his two companions stiffen, eyes wide with shock that anyone would dare be so rude to the Empress. Qing could have told them Master Zhi was equally outspoken with Chief Book Hunter Feng, who was a good two thousand years her senior—if not more—and one of the most powerful of his kind in all Khaitan.

Fortunately, the Empress didn't take offense, speaking in a soft, sweet voice. "Coming to you like this, hidden and alone, I can't expect to be treated as I would in our royal court. A-Zi, if you would?"

Eunuch Kang bowed and lifted the curtain between their rooms, revealing a smaller chamber with a variety of instruments on racks. The girl sitting at the center of the room, holding a pipa almost too big for her, looked barely old enough to be married, much less Empress of the An Kingdom. Her sleek black hair was pulled back tightly from rounded features and her eyes were huge and dark in her small face. Her robes were simple and almost too large for her small frame.

Immediately, Captain Li and his brother went to one knee, saluting the Empress. Kang Qiyun was a beat slower, too busy staring at the girl raptly to follow protocol. Meanwhile, Qing and Xinglu followed their masters' suit, cupping their hands and bowing deeply. As for Count Li, he merely inclined his head.

"Empress Ling Fei," Count Li said quietly. "Is it wise for you to wander outside the palace? Your husband is more than enough of a headache for me in these troubled times."

A pert little smile curved the Empress' lips. "Can we not waste breath on that nuisance? I wouldn't have taken the risk if I didn't think it was important." She turned her attention to Master Zhi. "I would have sent directly for you, but Eunuch Kang here is the only one I dare trust."

The claim elicited a scoff from Captain Li, one that earned the man a smug glance from Eunuch Kang. "I have certain advantages in that department," he murmured. "Not least of which having been raised at Empress Ling's side for most of her childhood."

To Qing's mind that begged the question, "But if that's the case, why aren't you her chief eunuch, instead of Eunuch Zhao?"

It was Kang Qiyun who answered, "Eunuch Zhao had seniority. Kang bro's just a year or so older than I am." At Eunuch Kang's long-suffering look, he added, "You said I can't call you that in the palace, bro. Never said a word about me not doing it in private."

There was no way to understand even half of the convoluted relationships involved here and Qing decided not to try. Instead he glanced at his master, knowing it wasn't his place to ask just what the Empress wanted. Fortunately for his intense curiosity, it was a feeling Master Zhi shared.

Making a slight coughing sound to draw everyone's attention, Master Zhi asked, "You came to meet me for a reason, Your Majesty. I doubt we've much time for you to speak. Perhaps you should do so now?"

"I should, yes." Empress Ling Fei smiled a bit weakly. "I've come to you because I couldn't tell my husband...."

"I am not a relationship guide, Your Majesty," Master Zhi pointed out. "My apprentice even less so. If you're hoping we can help you ensure an heir, I'm afraid you've come to the wrong person."

A soft laugh, weak and a little sad. "That isn't why I asked you here." Turning to the Count, she continued, "I'm told you received my scroll?"

"The one containing a portion of Pan Wei's *hun* soul?" Count Li asked dryly. "It's safely with his senior disciple now. But, Your Majesty, may I suggest that next time you wish to send me something of importance you send it to the Soul Protection Society? I spend precious little time in my mansion."

A startled flush of embarrassment crossed the Empress' face, quickly shifting to defensiveness. "I couldn't, though. Sending it to the Society would have been noticed. Whereas your secretary at the mansion is a cousin."

That explained how the scroll got where it was. It didn't explain why. Fortunately, the Empress continued, "My husband and I have to be careful when we meet in the palace. Eunuch Zhao keeps close watch on everything we say and do. Besides, that silly fool husband of mine thinks he can handle everything himself."

Count Li chuckled, "He does have a way of not listening, I admit. But I digress. Pan Wei explained some of why you sent me his scroll, but I'm assuming you have more to tell us?"

A sigh. "It started two months ago. I don't know the details, but my husband was attacked by a monster in his study. He... lost his left arm to it."

That made Kang Qiyun rub his arm in sympathy, even as he said, "All the more reason for you not getting involved, Your Majesty."

She scoffed. "Don't patronize me, you nuisance." She turned her attention back to Count Li. "Pan Wei told you about that, I'm sure. Told you I had him build my husband a new arm. But I knew that idiot wouldn't ask you for help because he never does. So I asked Pan Wei to try and contact you."

Master Zhi considered that. "A singularly poor choice of messenger, based on a few hours of knowing him."

"I was also concerned. Eunuch Zhao was searching for something in my chambers. I didn't want him to find Pan Wei's scroll. Gods know what he'd do with it."

"Ah. A better reason indeed. Perhaps you should have started with it?"

Undeterred, the Empress continued, "There's more. I'm certain that fire yesterday had something to do with what happened to my husband. Eunuch Kang, if you would?"

The eunuch bowed. "Of course, Your Majesty." He stepped forward, addressing Count Li again. "As one of their Majesties' personal bodyguard, it's my job to make sure everything around them remains safe. That means I have a number of information sources...."

"Spies," Captain Li muttered, causing Kang Qiyun and Li Aiqing to giggle.

"Very well. Spies. I have dozens throughout the palace. They report any odd situations to me, most of which are of no interest to anyone but myself and the spiders in the walls." A shrug. "Recently, however, Eunuch Zhao has been making an unexpected number of trips to the Imperial Mausoleum. I investigated the matter personally and while I found nothing obvious, I did notice some of his servants seemed poorly chosen. I requested Commander Fan investigate them."

Count Li frowned. "Was one bald, with a club foot?" At the eunuch's agreement, he sighed. "Number Three Baldy."

Master Zhi asked, "The Black Boulder Gang, then?"

Eunuch Kang spread his hands. "I believe so, based on what Commander Fan learned. I can't be certain, of course, because I've no idea what they did in the Imperial Mausoleum, but at a guess Eunuch Zhao found the place where that copy of the Pot of Ten Thousand Crows was hidden."

A thought occurred to Qing and he interrupted, "Eunuch Kang, what is the Imperial Mausoleum's layout?"

To the man's credit, he was unoffended. "The main hall, as you enter, holds the memorials for the current An dynasty. There are smaller halls off to the sides containing the memorials from previous dynasties: Ling, Sui, Kang, Qu, among others. It doesn't do to disrespect one's predecessors, no matter what you might think of them."

Qing understood that much. "You said Eunuch Zhao visited. Which halls did he go to?"

"I was told he paid respects to all except the Kang. Perhaps he didn't have time, or perhaps he isn't fond of them." Now the eunuch looked puzzled. "Does it matter?"

"He had the gang with him, but they didn't stop and do anything at the time?" At the still puzzled eunuch's agreement, Qing turned to his master. "Could he have known he was being watched? Could he have told the gang which hall to look for the Pot by not going to it? They wouldn't be able to read, after all."

Master Zhi's expression showed approval. "A convoluted thought. But this is a convoluted plot, made all the worse by palace politics."

The Empress spoke, "A-Zi, perhaps you should have someone investigate..." Her words broke off at a soft choked noise from Count Li. When they all looked his way, Qing realized the Count had stepped backwards, dark eyes shifting color to pale grey. A fine pattern of black and silver lines formed on his throat, as he said sharply, in familiar tones, "Get back to the Society now!"

Pang Hua, somehow using his brother to communicate.

CHAPTER 8
Hunting for the Truth

Zhi Wenku controlled, barely controlled, the urge to rush back to the Society without waiting for explanations. She was a Master Book Hunter and well past the age of running off thoughtlessly to deal with a crisis. Besides, it wouldn't do to give Qing ideas. Nor Xinglu, for that matter. Shen Wei grabbed his boy by his collar before he could so much as take a step.

When Count Li had control of his body again he took charge without wasting a moment. "Your Majesty, go home. It isn't safe. Captain Li, boys, you escort her and Eunuch Kang back. Quickly."

Though it looked like they wanted to argue, Count Li's tone and manner ensured they didn't. Instead, Eunuch Kang led his Empress and the other three away.

"What is it?" Zhi Wenku asked, once the others were out of earshot.

"Puppets like the ones who attacked Master Zhan's house are attacking the Society. My brother had just returned with that umbrella when they arrived. He's relatively sure they followed him." Count Li went to the window and pushed it open, stepping out onto thin air without hesitation. "Our defenses are holding, but I'm almost inclined to let them try taking what they want, as long as it isn't that key."

That almost seemed like a horrible idea. Almost. They might find their enemy's hiding place if they let the puppets take something less important and followed the things home. "What if they're after Master Zhan, or Pan Wei's scroll?" Zhi Wenku stepped onto her whisk and flew beside the Count, with the others following close behind.

"We'll keep them out of this, but I'm fairly sure the umbrella's harmless. The qi in it is too tangled up to be useful."

Zhi Wenku almost asked how the Count knew that, when he'd completely ignored the thing back at Zhan Ping's vault. She added the information to the growing pile of suspicions she'd been gathering ever since she'd met him and Pang Hua and continued, "What if it turns out the thing is useful?"

"We need to find the person behind this. Without a sense for where they are and what they're actually trying to accomplish, we aren't going to get anywhere."

The Count was right. Zhi Wenku didn't like letting an enemy have the thing they wanted but there were times when one had to give way in order to push forward. "Tell your brother that, then. Have him leave the Society with the umbrella. That way we'll know if that's what they're looking for, or something else."

Qing asked, "What if they split up?"

"If they split up, they wanted something else as well."

"I meant how do we deal with them, Master?"

Zhi Wenku glanced at Qing, whose eyes were wide and concerned. If it'd been Xinglu she'd have figured it for sass. With Qing, still innocent of such things—mostly innocent of such things—it would be an honest question. "Count Li, Master Shen and I give chase. You and Xinglu help fight off the puppets attacking the Society."

"You'll have my people's help." Count Li added, then pointed ahead at the Society's walls, where a familiar figure leapt over the rooftops, waving a closed and ragged umbrella in his left hand, his black umbrella in his right, spinning wildly as it carried him towards the river plains to their north. "You'll need it. The puppets are splitting up."

Dozens of familiar figures shambled away from the Society's walls, while another few dozen remained, trying to climb in and being broken by various members of the Society. It seemed to be a stalemate, because the puppets kept putting themselves back together.

"Is it my imagination or is the enemy getting stronger?"

"They're certainly more obstinate," Shen Wei noted. "Xinglu, you and Qing go help. We'll follow the ones chasing Pang Hua."

The boys were good apprentices. They didn't like being left out of the chase, but they obeyed orders. Zhi Wenku gave them an approving nod before turning her attention back towards Pang Hua as he bounced and sprang from rooftop to rooftop.

They followed behind, letting the puppets chase Pang Hua out of the city and into darkness of the river plain. It'd been just possible to see him and them in the city's dimly lit streets. Less easy outside the city, where the only light came from the stars gleaming bright in the sky.

Zhi Wenku automatically adjusted her vision for the darkness and knew her companions were doing the same. "Might have him lose the thing soon," she suggested. "Given you're serious about letting the enemy have it."

As if he'd heard the suggestion without needing Count Li to pass it on, Pang Hua suddenly tripped on nothingness and—indeed—dropped his 'treasure' into the river below. "Oops. Forgot about that," Count Li muttered for his brother. "Sorry."

Wondering why she was so often surrounded by humorists, because she was relatively certain Pang Hua had forgotten nothing of the sort, Zhi Wenku watched the puppets form a chain as they rushed into the river shallows and grabbed the artifact.

Then, to Zhi Wenku's surprise, they crossed the river and headed northeast. "Where are they going?" she asked quietly. "As far as I know, there's nothing but a few villages that way." She'd expected the things to stay closer to the city, but this suggested their controller was further away than she'd realized. If so, the enemy had an impressive range.

"Only one way to find out," Shen Wei said, turning his sword to follow, just as Pang Hua joined them. "Why the river?" he asked.

"Damn thing tried to bite me. I'd have dropped it even if we weren't planning on letting them have it." Pang Hua floated beside his brother, a shadowy twin who could not quite stop fluttering around as he flew. "I tore it in the process. We can use the piece I kept to scry for the rest, if we lose track."

Glancing at the piece of parchment in Pang Hua's hand, Zhi Wenku spotted a few words in oddly light ink written on what had to have been the umbrella's inner surface. The parchment was too wrinkled for her to make out what was written on the thing, but she made a mental note to find out later.

For now, however, they had an enemy to hunt down.

弟子

The walls of the Soul Protection Society were relatively tall compared to the surrounding buildings. They were also covered in a smooth material that made it difficult for most people to climb. Unfortunately, the invading puppets weren't most people. Constructed from leather and wood, with ivy growing between the cracks, their bodies bore only the slightest resemblance to human.

The ivy gave the puppets an edge when climbing the wall, gripping tight and growing upwards to pull the puppets behind. If the Society's disciples weren't skilled cultivators, hardly fazed by strange things attempting to break into their headquarters, there would have been no contest.

As it was, the biggest problem was the puppets' tenacity. They climbed and fell, climbed and fell and climbed again. They even repaired themselves as they went, ivy reweaving the leather and wood together.

"I don't care if they're her style, these can't possibly be Daoping's work," Qing muttered as he and Xinglu dealt with a puppet that'd gone around the corner, trying to sneak in without being noticed. Unfortunately for it, the two of them had arrived from that direction.

"Won't disagree with you," Xinglu said, cutting the thing's head off and crushing it thoroughly to keep it from reviving itself. "But why do you say that?"

"She's been dead over a century. Squash would be completely dried out by now." Qing gestured at the smashed vegetable matter leaking from the seams of the leather casing. "And they seem to need those to keep moving."

Even as he spoke, the damned puppet proved him wrong, righting itself and trying obstinately to climb the wall again, unperturbed by its missing head. "Or maybe not. Still, those squash are awfully fresh." They smelled good, too, reminding Qing that he hadn't eaten anything but snacks for a while.

"It could be a preservation spell." Xinglu suggested as he grabbed the puppet by the nape of its neck and pulled it down. "I think it needs torn apart. Whatever's animating it has to be somewhere."

A preservation spell was possible but unlikely. "If you're powerful enough to keep several dozen squash in good condition for a hundred or so years, you don't need these puppets to do your bidding. They're far too weak." Qing ripped the puppet's torso open, digging through the ivy for some sort of core. "Here it is."

'It' was a piece of carved wood covered in tiny words. Qing memorized them quickly, then crushed the carving to splinters, making sure to destroy it as thoroughly as possible. "That handwriting looks familiar," he muttered.

"We'll worry about that later. Best stop the other puppets before my cultivational siblings pull out the more dangerous weapons."

Qing could hardly guess what sort of dangerous weapons the Soul Protection Society could call upon, but he was sure they shouldn't be used in a crowded city. Based on what he'd seen of some of the Society's people, the probability that someone would forget sense was a bit too high.

Indeed, as he and Xinglu came around the corner they spotted a group of disciples, Senior Yao alongside them, shoving a huge pot towards the edge of the wall. Whatever it was, its contents glowed a pretty shade of pink and stank of something thick, heavy and quite sulfurous. It had to be a powerful stench, given they could smell it this far away.

"Oh shit," Xinglu muttered. "That's Master Shen's disposal tank."

"Go stop them. I'll deal with the puppets." Qing wasn't sure his master would approve of his plan but there were about too many puppets for him to readily handle without changing to his dragonling form. He did so, dashing alongside the wall to the cheers of the juniors above him, grabbing one puppet in his mouth, two each in all four of his claws, and two more wrapped in his tail.

Behind him, Xinglu set to shouting at his fellow Society members. "No. NO NO NO NO NO! Are you stupid?"

Qing ignored the argument, flying high above the city. Only when all he could see below him was the faintest of lights, only when the air went thin and cold, did he stop, hovering in place and gathering his *qi*.

He'd not rested enough for a proper storm. He didn't need a proper storm. All he needed was to burn the puppets down to their cores with one powerful bolt of lightning. The air went still for a moment, buzzing intensely. Then a snap of red energy flared around him, the natural forces of the atmosphere drawn to him by his internal *qi,* creating a huge and brief explosion.

The puppets smoldered in his grasp and went still. Qing waited several seconds longer to be sure they wouldn't move again, then flew back down, intending to help Xinglu with the last half-dozen puppets. Except by the time he got there, his friend had finished the fight.

He'd also gotten soaked in whatever was in that tank, to his obvious annoyance. Seeing Qing's expression and reading it despite him being a dragon, Xinglu grumbled, "Don't worry. Master Shen says I'm practically immune to most alchemy mistakes. A good thing too, given how many I make."

Qing didn't question his friend's assurance though he couldn't help worrying. He dropped the charred puppets and turned human so he could cover his nose. "If nothing else, you need a bath," he began, only to stop at a familiar sound.

Looking towards the noise, Qing was wearily unsurprised to see a small troop of Kirin Guard marching towards them, led by Commander Fan yet again. What did surprise him, however, was the elaborate palanquin at the center of the troop.

"Is that," he began.

"Yes," Xinglu agreed glumly. "That palanquin belongs to one man, and only one man may ride it."

As Commander Fan marched forward, clearly out of sorts with the whole situation, Qing wondered just what the Emperor wanted now.

The puppets moved fast. Too fast to trace by sight alone. If Pang Hua hadn't kept a piece of the stolen umbrella as a focus, they might have lost the trail entirely.

"When this is done," Zhi Wenku told the man, "I'd like to have a look at that thing." She gestured at the flapping piece of parchment flying ahead of them on a string; a ragged kite that'd seen far better days.

"I've no objection. Is there a reason?"

"There's writing on it. I'm a Book Hunter. Do I need a better reason?"

That surprised both Pang Hua and the Count, the latter of whom repeated, "Writing?"

"You didn't notice?" Zhi Wenku put an image of what she'd seen on her fan,

"I ONLY CAUGHT A GLIMPSE SHE ADMITTED."

the characters glowing in the darkness so her companions could see them.

The brothers frowned, obviously confused, and when Zhi Wenku raised a brow at their puzzlement, Shen Wei noted, "I didn't see them either. But you're a Master Book Hunter, my dear. I'm sure it's possible to hide words from you, but one would have to know to do so, first."

Ah. Yes. That was true. Zhi Wenku tended to forget that her training, her nature, made her especially sensitive to written words, no matter what means were used to create them, no matter what means were used to hide them. "I only caught a glimpse," she admitted. "But I feel as if they might be important."

"Given they were on that damned copy," Pang Hua grumbled, "they almost have to be."

By this time they'd crossed the river plain. The mass of mountains rising on the other side were too dark and solid to make out in this light, but Zhi Wenku thought she knew the direction they were headed. "Isn't that Fenghua Shan?" she asked suddenly, pointing ahead of them. They were northeast of Chang'an by now and that mountain was the one on her mental map of the region.

A pause while Count Li thought about it. "I think so, yes."

"Where Pan Wei's craft hall... I mean workshop... is hidden?"

Count Li frowned, the expression dimly visible to Zhi Wenku's dark-adjusted eyes. "Yes."

"Does it bother you as much as it does me that these puppets seem to be headed straight for it?"

Another moment of thought. "There's a certain sense to it, though. Everything that's happened so far has been related to that young fool's work."

"And Daoping's," Pang Hua noted. "She may have had another cache here that we didn't find. We should search around, once we've traced those puppets."

That agreed on, they flew a few minutes longer before finally landing on a flat and poorly tended stone platform overlooking a cliff. A small group of broken down buildings stood nearby, half-covered in weeds and bushes; the remnants of Pan Wei's craft village, no doubt. There was no light but puppets wouldn't need any. They didn't have proper eyes, after all.

Count Li and Pang Hua took lead, pale and dark reflections of each other. "I don't sense any life ahead," Count Li said. "If there's a cultivator here, they've done an excellent job of concealing... HELL!"

The last sounded more like Pang Hua, no matter whose lips it came from. Nor could Zhi Wenku blame either for their reaction because a stream of intense flame blasted towards them, nearly striking the pair. If the brothers had been lesser cultivators, they'd have been injured. As it was, the flames struck their quickly shifted umbrellas and set the nearby trees alight.

"What is it about fire?" Zhi Wenku complained, using her battle whisk to redirect the flames quickly. "At least there's no oil. Still, so destructive."

"That seems to be the point," Shen Wei suggested, moving to guard her back, his sword drawn and ready. "Puppets behind us, by the way."

That came as no surprise to any of them. Zhi Wenku waved off smoke with her fan, while Count Li and Pang Hua continued forward, blocking the flames as they moved. Shen Wei cut and sliced whatever came near, sword flying around him smoothly with every gesture.

"You aren't wanted here! Go away!"

Zhi Wenku frowned. The voice sounded like a child's, one barely old enough to be out at night, much less commanding fire and animated puppets to attack their enemy. It was also entirely unfamiliar. "Who is that?"

"You know, I don't know at all," Count Li admitted. "I can just see her behind the flames and she seems a bit young for this. Of course, it could be a disguise."

"Can you incapacitate her?"

"I'm not sure. Possibly? Depends on what she is. It's hard to tell at this point."

Zhi Wenku doused a few small fires. They were closer to the center of what had once been Pan Wei's enclave and was now a broken mess of stone buildings and weeds. It was the latter catching fire, though from what little she could see, there wasn't much left to burn.

The puppets behind them regenerated every time Shen Wei cut them down and Zhi Wenku pointed out, "You've destroyed that one's head and it's still trying to fight. I think its activator is probably in its chest."

"Like Zhu Kan's?"

The puppets Zhu Kan had created—when she and Shen Wei had first met— used cores formed of *qi* stolen from living beings. So far Zhi Wenku had sensed nothing similar in these puppets. "Not exactly. But the puppets need some sort of motive force and that has to be somewhere in their bodies."

"Ah. True." Shen Wei focused on striking the puppets' torsos, pin-cushioning the nearest one over and over again until it finally fell over. All while they kept moving towards the source of the flames.

By the time they reached the center of the ruins, Zhi Wenku could see the person attacking them. A little girl in tattered leather robes, covered in vaguely familiar markings. Her unbound hair flowed and rose behind her, resembling smoke, or wings, and her intense black eyes glared furiously at them from behind the leather and wooden fan she waved wildly between them.

"GO AWAY!" she shouted.

"Young lady, copy or not, the Five Fires and Seven Plume's Fan is not a toy," Count Li said. "Put it down and let us talk."

"NO!" She backed up, still waving her fan and casting gouts of flame. They moved towards her slowly, so as not to startle her, watching for traps on the ground ahead of them.

That last proved a mistake. The trap—when it came—turned out to have been hovering above, a miniature gold painted pagoda spinning in place. Zhi Wenku caught sight of it and shouted a warning a moment too late as the thing dropped down, enlarging as it landed, trapping them in darkness and near total silence.

Total silence, that was, except for Pang Hua cursing, "DAMNIT PAN WEI, WHY IN THE HELL DID YOU HAVE HER MAKE THE EXQUISITE PAGODA?"

弟子

The trouble with having the most responsible adults going off to be responsible elsewhere was that left far less responsible adults in charge. Qing couldn't tell the Society's leadership what to do, but he didn't think it was a good idea to obsequiously allow the Emperor inside their walls to hold conference with.

That, however, had been Senior Yao's immediate reaction. So immediate, in fact, that the various division heads didn't have a chance to countermand him. By the time they realized the Emperor and a whole troop of Kirin Guard were making themselves at home, the deed was already done.

"Makes one suspect Senior Yao of collusion," Qing muttered to Xinglu as the leaders hurriedly pretended to welcome the Emperor's presence. For all the Society might not want the Emperor there and didn't want him thinking he could command them, they also didn't want to create an incident.

"Frankly, it wouldn't surprise me." Xinglu pushed damp hair from his eyes, brows furrowed with irritation as they watched Master Xie of the Mechanist Section approach the Emperor. No deep bows or flowery speech, but polite and distantly welcoming, despite the lack of invitation. "He's stupid about some things, but he knows Chief Cultivator Li wouldn't allow this."

Commander Fan looked towards them, plainly irritated and ready to force better manners. Except the Emperor waved him off, focusing on his own purpose as he acknowledged Master Xie. "This Emperor was hoping to meet with the Chief Cultivator."

Qing frowned. Something about the man's voice seemed off. The man he'd met had sounded young but not quite so soft-voiced. Not having a good reason to say so, however, he held his tongue and watched carefully.

"Unfortunately, Chief Cultivator Li is busy elsewhere," the old man said in a quavering voice. It seemed certain the mechanist wasn't as enfeebled as he pretended.

"Then this Emperor will wait."

A soft murmur among the crowd of masters filling the room, as well as from the few disciples who'd slipped in before someone could tell them 'no'. They didn't like that idea at all. Unfortunately for them, short of actively throwing the Emperor out on his ear—a thing only Count Li would have been brave enough to do—their only recourse was to agree.

Xinglu yawned as the adults discussed—tried to discuss—the Emperor's intentions. "This is boring and could take all night," he grumbled. "And our masters have been gone forever."

"Forever is a complete exaggeration," Qing pointed out acerbically. "They've only been gone an hour, if that much."

"We could go after them."

Qing sighed. "No. Neither of our masters, or Count Li, would approve."

Xinglu looked like he wanted to insist even so. Except Qing remembered what Chief Cultivator Li had ordered them to do once they'd dealt with the puppets. "We're supposed to talk to Master Zhan and her friend, anyway."

"Oh. Yes. I forgot."

Qing would lay odds his friend had forgotten nothing of the sort. He didn't say so, just slid quietly out of the room with Xinglu close behind. To his annoyance, Commander Fan followed them, calling out with aggravation. They could have run but that would only make them look suspicious, especially to a man like Commander Fan.

They turned and bowed respectfully. "Commander," Xinglu said. "This apprentice greets you."

"You're Xinglu, right? Master Shen's apprentice? And you're Qing?"

"That's right," Xinglu said, looking confused. Not that Qing blamed him. Commander Fan had been introduced to Qing earlier that day and knew Xinglu by sight. So why did he act as if he didn't know either of them, now? He eyed the Commander, seeing nothing different about him.

But wait, there was one thing new. A leather belt that didn't fit Commander Fan's uniform, its surface covered in decorative designs too small to see without staring rudely. Qing regretted Captain Li's absence. The man would surely know if there was something odd there.

Commander Fan continued, "I'm of the understanding that Zhan Ping, the owner of the mansion that burned down, is staying at the Society's Headquarters."

Qing had to wonder why the man wanted to know. They surely weren't related. "She might be."

"Are you going to see her?"

"Why would we do that, sir?" Xinglu asked, sounding puzzled. "We've had a busy day and haven't eaten yet. We don't have time...."

A sudden motion. A red-tinted flash that left the imprint of raging fire against the back of Qing's eyes. A grab, catching Qing by the throat, spinning him around, dragging him back against the Commander's chest. "Make time," the Commander ordered, one arm crushed against Qing's windpipe, free hand clutching a sword that writhed and squirmed beneath its surface, a fiery dragon twisting in barely controlled rage.

Xinglu took a step towards the Commander, but the man raised his sword towards Qing's throat. "If you don't want your friend here skewered and baked from within, you'll lead me to Zhan Ping. Now."

Xinglu hesitated. Glanced at Qing. Sighed. "Very well, Commander Fan. I'll do as you ask." With that, he turned and led the way through the halls, not bothering, not needing, to make sure he was being followed.

CHAPTER 9
Capture and Escape

While Pang Hua raged and Count Li quietly sat in the middle of their prison, ignoring his brother's curses, Zhi Wenku and Shen Wei carefully examined the walls and floor.

"The walls are hardened leather, plain and unmarked," Shen Wei said from his side of the chamber, shining a night pearl on the wall. "They're fairly tall. I'd fly up, but something's blocking my *qi*."

"Mine as well." Zhi Wenku noted. "Pang Hua, you're in my way. If you aren't going to be useful, could you at least not be obstructive?"

"Ah, yes. Sorry, my good woman." Pang Hua stepped back from where he'd been banging on the walls, then returned to cursing furiously at their captor. He had a truly amazing command of the invective, with words and terms that hadn't been used for some thousands of years.

Shoving aside her curiosity again, Zhi Wenku ran her fingers along the bottom edge of the wall, where it met the floor. "Wood here. This is obviously another of Daoping's creations. Count Li, do you think you and your brother could break us out of here?"

"I doubt this copy is as strong as I am. I can bore a hole any direction you'd like. Would you like me to do so right now?"

The fact that he hadn't immediately acted to free them said he felt it risky. He was likely right. "Not yet. Let's finish examining the thing first."

Shen Wei's fan showed a mountain demon leaping out of a cauldron and straight into a fire. At her grin of agreement, he said, "The interior of this thing is fairly solid, despite being made of leather. I can't cut it with my sword or burn a hole in it with acid."

No surprise Shen Wei carried acid with him. He was an alchemist, after all, and one never knew what one might need. "What of the floor?"

"Also beyond my ability to harm."

Zhi Wenku peered around them, gazing slowly upwards to the dim shadows above. Now that was interesting. "I just spotted a faint light up there. Count, can you fly me to the top of this chamber so I can examine it?" Her *qi* might be limited in this place, but his surely wasn't. Not if he could use it to break them out.

"That I can, my dear lady." Count Li rose and took her hand, using his parasol to lift them both up into the darkness. Down below, the lights from the few night pearls they'd taken out resembled stars reflected on water. Above, the only light came from a single spot.

The walls drew closer the higher they went, wooden struts marking where the floors of the pagoda would be if the thing weren't hollow. "Pang Hua called this thing a copy of the Exquisite Pagoda? That would be the one carried by the Immortal Li Jing?"

"Yes."

The Immortal Li Jing had been given the Exquisite Pagoda to subdue his rebellious son, Nezha. If this were the real thing, escape would be nearly impossible. Given its probable creator, however, she suspected it had a weak point. One they might be able to exploit.

Carried to the highest point in the pagoda, Zhi Wenku examined their first possible escape. There was a hole in the very top, its edges tattered and blackened, an opening just big enough for something small to pass through. Zhi Wenku's diminished *qi* didn't prevent her from accessing her Warehouse. She'd several tools she could use to send a message to Qing.

She considered the possibilities. It wasn't much of a hole, ragged and dark as if it'd been beaten on and torn at before. She peered through it, spotting pale sky and a bird flying in the distance. Had they really been in there so long? It'd only felt like a few minutes, and yet it was already day?

"It's big enough for a messenger bird," Zhi Wenku muttered. "But I don't know."

"What's wrong?"

"I just don't like it." Zhi Wenku pointed. "Let's talk to the others."

They drifted down and as soon as they landed, Zhi Wenku dropped to one knee to examine the floor carefully. Then she used her fan to say, [[I think we should break through here.]]

"Eh?" All three men blinked at her, clearly puzzled.

[[The hole in the top has burn marks.]] she explained. [[I don't think I want anything to do with an escape that shows signs of fire damage.]]

Shen Wei went a little pale. [[No,]] he agreed.

Count Li borrowed Shen Wei's fan to ask, [[I can bore a hole any direction, but wouldn't the walls be better?]]

[[I don't want the enemy seeing us escape. If you can dig a hole in the ground deep enough, we can tunnel our way to freedom before they realize.]]

Count Li considered that carefully. Handed Shen Wei's fan back to him. Spun his parasol between his fingers. Then shoved the thing's struts backwards so it formed a cone. He aimed it at the floor, sending a beam of jet black energy down into the wooden surface, sucking the flooring and the stone beneath into the umbrella.

There was a scream of pain and the entire pagoda rocked. At the same time Count Li refolded his parasol and caught Zhi Wenku's hand before jumping down into the hole, drifting down slowly. Pang Hua followed suit with Shen Wei. All while the source of the scream sobbed and shrieked hysterically.

The hole was smooth as glass, cut through the living rock of the mountain. It was also damned dark, so their only light came from their night pearls. As Zhi Wenku's eyes adjusted she realized there was another light below, not far away and getting closer. She tensed, worried. They'd escaped one problem, yes, but had they fallen into another trap entirely?

And if so, who was behind it?

弟子

Master Zhan had been sent to stay in a guest house towards the back of the Society's grounds, one of a series of wooden buildings built cozily close; a small warren of elegant design. Cherry trees, just visible in the lamplight, swayed to a non-existent breeze, petals scattering with every movement. Below them, the water in the pond in the central courtyard reflected a full moon's light despite there being none in the sky.

Qing corrected himself. There was no moon in the sky above Chang'an. But the guest house existed in a small pocket of unreality, so what had been autumn outside was sweet spring inside. Someone had gone to some trouble to make the place comfortable and pleasant. But then, it was a guest house.

"Stop daydreaming!" Commander Fan nudged Qing forward sharply as Xinglu went ahead of them, striding towards the only building with any lights.

Allowing himself to be pushed forward, Qing analyzed his situation. He and Xinglu had cooperated to learn what Commander Fan was up to. It wasn't time to act. Not yet, but soon. He deliberately stumbled closer to the edge of that pond.

"Stop fiddling around!" Commander Fan ordered. "Where is she?"

"I'm sure Xinglu went to fetch her, Commander," Qing offered reassuringly, flinching back from the sword in Commander Fan's hand. He wanted a better look at the writhing fiery shape inside the blade. A dragon of some sort? The blade glittered like metal, but now Qing realized it was wood painted with some shiny substance. "Wouldn't it be better to forge a sword from iron?"

The arm around his neck tightened sharply and its owner snapped. "It's none of your business what I use."

What he used? So Commander Fan was an artificer as well? Or was there more to it than that? Qing remembered Master Zhan's lecture earlier that day. She'd been telling those students to start with two materials, one rigid, one malleable. Her materials were apparently stone and wood and some others Qing hadn't noticed.

Pan Wei's base materials were clearly paper and metal. And everything Daoping had created appeared to incorporate leather and wood. There'd been ivy and squash as well, but perhaps they were an offshoot of wood? If the sword was her work that meant Commander Fan was involved with her or with what she'd left behind. But that didn't explain the fire.

Oh, but wait. Master Zhan had also said that as an artificer improved their skill, the more materials they'd want to choose. She'd even suggested Master Pan incorporated air in his creations. Could Daoping have incorporated fire?

Once again Commander Fan shook Qing. "Don't fall asleep on me, boy. I want your complete attention."

Qing ignored the criticism. "How did you get fire to work with wood and leather? Wouldn't it burn them up?"

Another shake. Qing was getting very tired indeed of being shaken. Snarling, clearly at the end of his patience, Commander Fan said, "Because I'm just that good."

"Nonsense. Daoping was never as good as she claimed she was. If you insist on following in her footsteps, you're not going to get any further than she did." Master Zhan came out of her guest house, robe hastily tied, grey hair frazzled around her tired face. Xinglu stood behind her, looking grimly determined. Any minute he'd turn hound so he could tear Commander Fan's throat out.

"Silence!" The sword that'd been perilously close to Qing's neck moved to point towards Master Zhan. "I'll take your head from your shoulders like I took your arm!"

Master Zhan stared with an expression of confusion. "You weren't even born when I lost my arm," she protested.

"SHUT UP!" The Commander shook Qing sharply, mostly for emphasis. "Where's the key?"

"What key?"

"The key to our master's craft hall!"

Predictably, that set Master Zhan raging. "MASTER PAN'S CRAFT HALL WAS DESTROYED!"

"IT WAS NOT! GIVE ME THE KEY!"

Qing was beginning to get an inkling of what might be going on. It was a fantastic idea but no more fantastic than anything he'd experienced so far. He let his captor shake him, fingers sliding around to catch at Commander Fan's belt. No surprise to find it gone. He'd a pretty good idea where it actually was.

"THE HELL YOU THINK YOU'RE DOING, LITTLE BOY!" Commander Fan shouted in his ear, shaking him yet again, so hard a human boy's neck might have snapped. "STOP SQUIRMING!"

Obeying to give himself time to work out his next move, Qing hung in Commander Fan's grip. Spotting Xinglu about to act, Qing hurriedly raised a hand to hold him off. Then, as Master Zhan and the man argued over the existence—or non-existence—of Pan Wei's craft hall, he shifted to his smallest dragon form, snatched the sword from Commander Fan's hand, and dove straight into the depths of the fishpond.

All while hoping Xinglu would know that he could, and should, act now.

弟子

They landed lightly in a passageway built of smooth grey metal and lit by what looked like enough night pearls to finance a dynasty. Releasing Zhi Wenku, Count Li sheathed his umbrella at his back and gazed around with interest. "This is familiar."

"Master Pan Wei's workshop?"

"En. I believe so. Lucky thing I stopped cutting when I felt the hole." Count Li stepped out of the way to let his brother land with Shen Wei. "Might want to close that up."

"Don't need to tell me that once, you know."

"I know, but it amuses me to do so."

As the brothers squabbled genially, Pang Hua turned his umbrella inside out and released a stream of stone that rose up into the hole they'd escaped through. The same stone Count Li's umbrella had just swallowed? Zhi Wenku was sure of it.

Noting her interested look, Count Li told her, "You suspected they were connected already, I'm sure."

"I did. I wasn't absolutely certain." Zhi Wenku checked Shen Wei before asking, "Which way do we go?"

"I wouldn't know, really." Count Li examined their surroundings more carefully. "Pan Wei's workshop is something of a rabbit warren. Full of little traps for intruders that he was always falling into himself."

No surprise there. She couldn't help muttering, "Was he a Khaitan Tu?" The clan was known for their talent for creating devices and causing trouble for those around them. Not out of any desire to harm, but just out of sheer mischief and curiosity.

"I've long suspected it, though he claimed not every time I asked." Count Li chuckled wryly at the memory. "In any event, our only hope is to keep moving and try to go upwards to the main entrance. There's probably some hidden exits scattered around this place but good luck finding them."

That made sense and Zhi Wenku pulled out her little dragonfly charm, telling it, "Go up the hall and come back. Tell me what you find."

As the device zipped one direction, then the other, Shen Wei pulled out a bottle of restorative and handed it to her. "We've been working non-stop for hours now and while we both practice fasting, that's no excuse for not repleni...." He broke off as the wall nearest them suddenly reached out a metal arm and snatched the bottle from him.

The bottle glugged briefly, then clattered to the floor while they stared. "What the hell just happened?" Pang Hua demanded.

Immediately, Zhi Wenku lashed her whisk, intending to catch hold of whatever invisible or camouflaged being had pranked them. Except its strands struck the once more flat metal and slid down, catching nothing. "It got away."

Something giggled in her ear and she thought she saw movement out of the corner of her eye. Again she lashed out. Again she missed, even as the giggles faded.

"Remember what I said about Pan Wei's traps?" Count Li said evenly, "This may be one of them."

Near as Zhi Wenku could tell, it was trying to bait them into following. When her dragonfly reported that the opposite direction was both clear and had a set of stairs going up, she said, "Pan Wei's *hun* soul seemed a nice enough fellow but that doesn't mean his traps are safe to play with. Let's ignore that... whatever it was... and go the other way."

The other three agreed and they headed up to what was hopefully the next level, then on and on and interminably on through a maze of twisted passages. Shen Wei attempted to mark the path, but that didn't help; something kept turning the markings around. Whatever it was even turned the arrows to point straight up twice, straight down twice, left and right—again twice, then one on the floor and one on the roof of the passage.

"This is worse than Khaitan's royal cavern," Zhi Wenku complained. "Does it really think we're going to follow its advice?"

Again something giggled and again Zhi Wenku caught sight of movement somewhere ahead of them. This time it wasn't invisible or the same color as the wall. Instead it was a human figure standing elegantly at the far end of the passage, blocking one of two openings. Human shaped, but not human, Zhi Wenku realized as they drew closer. A faceless thing of black and white paper and wire, a parasol of the same material spinning negligently in its fingers.

Zhi Wenku glanced at Count Li, who had a long-suffering expression, then at Pang Hua who just looked amused. Apparently the obvious—incredibly obvious—reference to the pair of them was less irritating than being trapped by a copy of the Exquisite Pagoda.

"So," she asked quietly, "Do we fight our way past? Or let the damned fool lead us where it wants us to go after all?"

弟子

The koi pond steamed from the heat of the sword Qing had stolen and he nearly flung himself back into the air, afraid of harming the fish. Except the water never grew warmer than a sunlit pond, its temperature controlled by whatever spell had created this place.

The sword in Qing's foreclaws struggled to break free, its malleable surface bending and twisting wildly. It shrieked with wordless fury, a blast of mental energy slamming into Qing's thoughts and trying to take them over. If Qing weren't a Book Hunter it might have succeeded.

Having spent years dealing with dangerous books, particularly the self-aware kind, Qing was accustomed to protecting his mind. Lacking words, the sword only had its intense, inchoate, desire to drive its attack. And its intense, inchoate, desire was aimed at something Qing lacked entirely; a craving for power over others.

Somewhere above came a shout of confused rage, followed by Xinglu's water-muffled howl. Qing wasn't sure his friend needed to attack Commander Fan but it'd be just as well to keep the man from involving himself with Qing's fight. He did hope his friend wouldn't hurt his opponent, though. He was fairly sure Commander Fan wasn't a willing participant in this situation.

Noticing Master Zhan leaning over the pond, peering curiously into the water, Qing lifted his head so he could ask, "Is there any special way to destroy Daoping's work?"

"Daoping?" A thoughtful expression crossed the woman's face, then amusement as Qing was pulled back down into the water to struggle with the captured sword again. When he surfaced she said, "If that thing's her copy of the Flaming Belt Sword, then you're doing it."

Doing it? Oh. "You mean keeping it in the water?"

"Well, isn't it obvious, little dragon? Water douses fire."

Tugged back down, Qing had to admit she was right. The sword did seem to be getting weaker. Just not fast enough for him. He managed to get his head above water and asked, "Anything quicker?"

"Destroy the maker's mark?"

Dragged down and sent spinning around the edges of the pond now, Qing wanted to shout with frustration. How in the name of all the Gods was he supposed to find the maker's mark on something that kept twisting and bending and struggling in his claws?

A particularly rough spin sent a wave splashing out of the pond, causing both Xinglu and Commander Fan to shout "HEY!" in near perfect unison. The wave had soaked them through, it seemed. The fish below weren't too happy about things either.

Qing ignored everyone, trying to work out what to do. He struggled to examine the sword, shifting his vision so he could see everything drawn and written on the thing. No words in a language he knew, but recalling how his friend Cui Wen marked his pieces with stylized clouds, he guessed Daoping's mark would be similar.

Once again he managed to get his head above water and shout, "What's the reading of her name?"

An amused drawl. "You could just ask what the mark is, you know. It's a jade knife."

Dragged back underwater, Qing recalled that one of the readings for 'ping' was jade. He searched the sword's surface and spotted the character written in talismanic script, framed inside a butcher's knife. The discovery made the sword set to spinning around in earnest, taking Qing around with it.

That didn't stop Qing, though it did make him terribly dizzy. He clutched the sword, using his thumb claw to scratch deeply across the mark, ruining it entirely. There was a final raging shriek, then the sword went silent and still, though Qing still spun around several times further, unable to stop himself.

At last he pulled his head up and out of the water and leaned against the edge of the pond. "I think I'm going to be sick," he muttered as Master Zhan knelt beside him. Her hand was light on his brow, almost as kind as Master Zhi's could be when he'd done well.

"GET OFF ME, YOU MONSTER! YOUR BREATH STINKS, YOUR WHOLE SELF STINKS AND YOU WEIGH TOO MUCH!"

That was Commander Fan, who lay beneath an amused and now calm Xinglu, who'd apparently concluded the commander wasn't enough of a threat to fight. Both were soaked from head to toe and Qing hoped they'd forgive him for splashing them.

Qing dragged himself out of the water after a good minute of heavy breathing. He was exhausted and didn't have time to admit it. "I think Commander Fan is safe," he told his friend. "The sword controlled him."

Xinglu considered that. "It explains why he was too confused to fight," he admitted. "All right. I'll let him up." He stood, shaking himself off thoroughly before changing to his human form. "Are you all right?"

Qing curled up on the nearest rock. "I shouldn't have taken my smallest form," he grumbled. "That thing had me spinning around like a bamboo dragonfly." He gestured with a hind claw at the sword, lying still and silent on the pond's edge. Whatever had made it so lively earlier seemed to have been thoroughly defeated, thankfully. "Sorry about splashing you."

Commander Fan opened his mouth to shout again but Master Zhan turned and glared before he could say a word. "You came in here holding that boy hostage," she snapped. "Don't you dare raise your voice to any of us."

It took the man a moment. "I wasn't in control," he admitted much more softly, almost sounding embarrassed. "I couldn't stop it."

Qing stretched his spine, cracking every joint from tail tip to the back of his skull. Oh, that did feel good. Realizing the Commander was watching him with wide and—oh dear—admiring eyes, he remembered too late how these people reacted to dragons. "I'm not a God," he said quickly.

"You're a dragon, though! A real dragon!"

"This isn't the time," Xinglu grumbled. "And why can't you people revere demon dogs instead? I'd be waist deep in treats if you revered demon dogs."

Unable to keep from laughing, Qing almost fell off the rock. At the same time Master Zhan asked, "Could you tell us what happened, Commander Fan?"

The Commander opened his mouth, about to answer, when a thought seemed to occur to him. "Not yet," he said, sounding worried. "We have to get back to the main building."

"Why?"

"Because the man I brought here isn't the Emperor. It's Eunuch Zhao, and he's the one who gave me that sword."

Qing and Xinglu looked at each other and, without hesitation, set off running.

CHAPTER 10
Another Broken Soul

"To be honest, Master Zhi, I don't know our best choice. That's clearly Pan Wei's work, but at this point I can't be sure we can trust it any more than we can trust anything related to that whole business." Count Li shook his head at the figure blocking the one path. All while the other was completely unprotected.

The paper figure danced around, making sassy gestures, as if it thought it was the Monkey King instead of yet another representation of the World Umbrella. It was damned obvious what the copied artifact wanted and equally uncertain whether they should cooperate.

Zhi Wenku considered the question. Considered the path they'd taken thus far. It'd seemed to be going up, which surely would be the right direction to reach the exit. And yet. And yet. "I get the impression Pan Wei liked to play games with people?"

"Mm. He loved them. The more confusing the better." Pang Hua grinned, adding, "One of the things I liked best about him, really."

Yes, well, he would. From long experience, Zhi Wenku knew the best way to avoid getting caught in a trickster's game was not to play it. But right that moment she had to wonder if they were already entangled. Follow the puppet and be led by the nose to whatever it was it wanted from them? Or choose some other path and just keep going up?

She eyed the puppet, knowing she'd get no help or advice from the brothers. Shen Wei would be more forthcoming, but he looked as worried as she felt, and as unsure of their choices. "How well did Pan Wei know you two? I'm guessing enough to poke fun at your weapons."

A chuckle. "He poked fun at everyone who came near him," Count Li agreed. "I won't say we were close. He was quite stubbornly busy trying to raise his cultivation to the next level."

"So, if he wanted to protect something from thieves, would he put obvious guardians in their path? Or would he hide it and make it seem like part of the architecture?"

"Of the two? The latter."

That was what Zhi Wenku thought. At last she said, "Follow it."

Shen Wei raised a brow. "I would never argue with the expert in such matters, but is there a reason? It isn't wise to let a potential enemy play the tune we dance to. Even if the thing's trying to keep us from going near Pan Wei's workshop, surely it won't lead us straight to the exit."

Walking towards the puppet blocking their path, causing it to slowly back up as if it meant to run, Zhi Wenku agreed. "Remember what I said about some books or scrolls absorbing their creators' personalities? About how some, more powerful ones, become semi-sentient?"

"You've said the really powerful books could become human," Shen Wei agreed, though he still looked puzzled. "What does that have to do with things?"

"It's true of artifacts as well. So this puppet isn't just following the patterns designed for it by its creator, but acting in its creator's stead. And that means—I hope—that it's trying to lead us out, or somewhere safe. In the most annoying way possible, of course, but consider its creator."

The puppet did a backflip. Danced around foolishly, folding and unfolding and reversing its umbrella in imitation of both the Count and Pang Hua. If nothing else, the behavior relieved Shen Wei's mind. "You may be right, my dear."

They followed the puppet down a set of stairs. Down more. Up a flight and another flight, then left and right and left and right yet again, until it came to a wall where it poked two seemingly meaningless spots. As a passage opened into a short and dimly lit tunnel downwards, Shen Wei asked, "If it's leading us to the exit then why in the world are we going down? Surely we should be headed up?"

To be honest, Zhi Wenku had no idea. Except she remembered the way those arrows they'd drawn had shifted position earlier. She reminded her companions, adding, "I think the place's defenses were trying to tell us which way to go from the first. The path we just followed is the same."

The puppet turned and made a gesture of approval, then led them through the short passage to a small metal door that opened into a small grotto, surrounded by pines. The first dim light of a summer morning shone against dew soaked trees.

A faint shimmer in the air above them told Zhi Wenku things weren't what they appeared. They hadn't been walking around long enough for the sun to be rising. "A side-space?" she asked, suddenly reminded of Khaitan's Royal Garden.

The puppet bowed politely, gesturing forward, towards a blue clad figure sitting on the edge of the balcony overlooking the mountainside. Zhi Wenku hesitated. Glanced at Count Li to see if he wanted to take over and—when he chose not to—continued forward.

"MASTER PAN WEI ?"

Their host—and Zhi Wenku had no doubt he was their host—turned, revealing pale features that flickered and faded with every movement. "My apologies," he said slowly, in a hoarse whisper. "My creations will play."

"Master Pan Wei?" Zhi Wenku asked gently, certain this was another part of the man's *hun* soul.

"Is that my name? It feels like it should be. But I'm not good with names."

"If they're difficult for you, we needn't bother with them. We came to your place here by accident...."

"Not an accident."

The statement startled them and Shen Wei repeated, "Not an accident? Who's doing, then? Yours? Or someone else's?"

A slow, thoughtful, look. "I don't think I did it. I don't remember doing it. But I don't remember much of anything. Ah... what was I saying?"

"Don't ask too many questions at once," Zhi Wenku suggested. She focused on the important question. "Is there a way out of here?"

"I... don't think you want to do that. I... think... she's waiting for you to do that. I think you'll be burned if you do that."

She. Remembering the 'child' that'd trapped them inside the pagoda, Zhi Wenku could only guess that she was the one involved. The voice that'd screamed when they'd forced their way out the pagoda's flooring had sounded like a woman as well. A woman or yet another little girl?

Turning to her companions, Zhi Wenku asked, "Do any of you have something to help a *hun* soul recover itself?"

Clearly remembering what the Pan Wei in the scroll had said about his *hun* soul being split, Shen Wei asked, "Which part of his *hun* soul do you think this is? Each one has different requirements."

At a guess, the *hun* soul in Pan Wei's scroll governed intellect. That meant this was either Pan Wei's liveliness or emotion. Of the two, the latter seemed most likely. Zhi Wenku said as much, adding, "He was executed just outside his door here. Anything he left behind would be traumatized."

Shen Wei considered that. "In that case, I recommend a *yang* restorative. If I have the ingredients I can make one up right away."

They hardly had time. They also hardly had a choice. "Of course, my dear," she told him. "As quickly as ever you can." It was testament to how seriously Shen Wei regarded the situation that he didn't retort that he was an alchemist, not a miracle doctor.

弟子

It only took a few minutes to reach the Society's main building and only a minute more to get past the guards. They knew better than to argue with a dragon who'd forgotten to turn human and the demon dog apprentice to one of their Masters.

When they ran into the meeting hall their fears were proved right. Almost everyone in the room cowered against the far wall, the stench of burned meat thick in the air. Two or three guards lay on the ground around the table, clearly injured, possibly dead. At the same time, Senior Yao and several others struggled to block more flames with arrays and weapons.

In the center of the room, swarming like mating serpents, a ball of dragon-like creatures glowed and smoked with inner fire. There were nine of them, Qing was sure, recalling the details from Master Zhi's book. "That would be a copy of the Shroud of Nine Fiery Dragons," he muttered into Xinglu's ear.

"An awfully small Shroud of Nine Fiery Dragons," Xinglu muttered back. "Maybe for a rat?"

This drew the fake Emperor's attention and Qing sensed the man hidden behind his costume glaring at Xinglu, only to pause and stare wildly at Qing. "...a... a dragon...?"

These people really needed to learn the difference between Heavenly dragons and a youngster like Qing. All things considered, he was glad he wasn't the sort to take such matters seriously. Not that Master Zhi would have let him if he'd so much as pretended to be anything more than a dragonling and apprentice Book Hunter.

Still, this might be the best time to make use of the local customs. Qing flew off Xinglu's shoulder, tripling his size. As the 'Emperor' stared, Qing focused his attention on the fiery dragons in the center of the room. He'd have to fight its wielder if he grabbed the shroud itself. There wasn't time. Senior Yao and his compatriots were faltering.

Darting forward, Qing spun around the fiery ball at high speed, drawing water and air and thunder together around him as he circled and circled and circled the 'dragons', building a sphere of chill mist too damp and too full of lightning to be burned away by the relatively weaker flames. Then he pulled the sphere tight; dampening the flames, cutting off their air.

As he worked, he caught glimpses of Xinglu battling the 'Emperor', their swords clashing loudly as they struck and parried and struck again. He'd have cheered for his friend's skill but he had to focus. The last thing they needed was for the dragons to break free and set the whole room alight. They'd done quite enough harm already.

Quite suddenly the fiery dragons were gone. Not destroyed by Qing's efforts but by Xinglu having sliced their source into pieces with several strikes of his black sword. Qing released his power and landed on the table. He couldn't take his human form. The fake Emperor didn't know Qing was a dragon. Best not reveal the truth now.

"You dare raise weapons to your Emperor?" the man demanded.

"You dare pretend to be this Emperor?" a new voice said from the doorway. When Qing turned to look, he saw another man—dressed in the exact same robes—striding into the room.

Captain Li and his little brother entered next, along with two Royal Guards. Neither Li spoke, just stepped forward and caught the fake by the shoulders, forcing him to his knees before anyone could so much as react.

The new man, the real Emperor, gestured for his guards to assist the task. "This Emperor is disappointed in you," he said calmly. "Captain Li, remove his headgear. Prove to everyone who this man is."

A quick motion tugged the cloth mask from the man's face, revealing Eunuch Zhao. Commander Fan had been right. Zhao was pallid, face damp with sweat, eyes full of fear. "Please! This Servant could not control! This Servant was under a spell! This Servant...."

"This Emperor will deal with you later," the Emperor said grimly. "You've a fondness for imprisoning people. I think it's high time you had a similar experience in Eunuch Kang's dungeons. Commander Fan, take him away."

The Commander saluted as he entered the room behind the others, his Kirin Guards close behind. "This Servant obeys," he said calmly.

As Commander Fan dragged his prisoner off the Emperor turned to Qing. "I've just been informed Fenghua Shan is burning, Qing. Given the fondness the one behind our problems has for fire, this Emperor suspects your Master may be in trouble there. Suggest you go to her aid, before something goes terribly wrong."

Qing glanced at his friend, who nodded, pushing the window open so they both could leap out into the night and go after their masters. All while Qing wondered and wondered just how the Emperor realized who he actually was.

弟子

As Shen Wei set up his cauldron and went through his materials, Zhi Wenku went to look out across the landscape. Alchemy wasn't something she understood and while she didn't mind learning, she also didn't want to put any pressure on him.

"I never knew Pan Wei had a side-space." Count Li and his brother joined her at the railing, their features all the more identical in the soft light. "Though he helped design the one we use for guests back at the Society, so I suppose it isn't a surprise."

"He must have used the same techniques inside his scroll," Zhi Wenku answered. "And now I wonder if he had anything to do with the design of Khaitan's Royal Gardens. If so, he really needs to learn to change his secret passages up."

Pang Hua looked puzzled. "I don't quite understand."

"The paths we took to get here followed a pattern. You remember me saying it was the same pattern our guide made our arrows follow?" At Pang Hua's agreement, Zhi Wenku continued wryly, "The Royal Gardens grotto used that pattern as well, though I believe they changed it after some thieves got in."

After a moment of consideration, Count Li murmured, "He never went to Khaitan, but I believe his master, Kang Huang did."

The name reminded Zhi Wenku of another small question that'd occurred to her. "That boy—Kang Qiyun—is he a descendant of Kang Huang's?"

A terribly amused expression crossed Count Li's face. "He is, via a concubine's daughter. She married out and took her new family's name."

Now Zhi Wenku was puzzled. A concubine's daughter had little in the way of legal rights. And if she married out of the family, then, "How is it he goes by the name of Kang, then?"

"Oh, that?" Count Li was about to explain when something made the ghostly *hun* soul of Pan Wei rise from his place and stare down the mountainside. "What is it?"

Realizing how odd it was for the broken *hun* soul to react so strongly, Zhi Wenku peered through the trees and boulders towards the perpetual dawn rising in the distance. For a moment she saw nothing of note, no reason whatsoever to draw the spirit's attention. Then she spotted a faint flicker amid the trees, off towards the south.

She focused her sight and slowly realized the peaceful image of serene forest was cracking. Worse, the edges of those cracks glowed red and gold, fading to black, like a painting set alight from behind. "Fire," she said grimly. "Again, fire."

"Shouldn't have used fire," Pan Wei's *hun* soul murmured. "Not strong enough to handle."

"You mean Daoping?"

The *hun* soul's face went whiter than it'd been before. "Daoping, don't. Please. You're a good girl. Don't." His hand went to his throat, as if trying to hold himself together and he nearly collapsed, unable to handle the memory.

Shen Wei put a pill in the *hun* soul's mouth. "He needs more than this, but it'll have to do for the moment. The poor man must have been devastated by her betrayal."

That much was painfully obvious. It was also painfully obvious someone—Daoping or her successor—intended to follow the artificer's path and ruin what little was left of Pan Wei's legacy. "Is it that fan again?"

"Most likely. I doubt the pot has recovered enough to release more crows," Pang Hua agreed. "Damnit. How did we manage to miss so many of her works?"

"This isn't the time to concern ourselves with that," Count Li pointed out. "The weather's been too dry and the whole mountain will be burning at this rate. I don't think it can get inside Pan Wei's workshop, but there are farms and villages nearby. We may have to risk our power making things worse."

Remembering the Count's concern that he and his brother's full power could be devastating, Zhi Wenku turned her attention on the puppet standing at the side-space's entrance, performing tricks with its umbrella. "Are there fire fighting tools in this place?"

The puppet tilted its head. Looked at its master, who nodded weakly. Then the thing spun around, heading for the exit, clearly confident she'd follow.

Leaving Shen Wei to continue his work, Zhi Wenku and the brothers followed the puppet on a convoluted path that had absolutely no pattern Zhi Wenku could recognize, until they reached a large room full of the scattered remnants of Pan Wei's experiments. This wasn't the time to be distracted, but Zhi Wenku noticed huge scraps of paper plastered to the walls, covered in Pan Wei's writing. She recognized a fan similar to the ones she and Shen Wei carried, as well as other interesting and intricate items that she didn't have time to record.

The puppet opened a pair of metal doors, revealing dozens of paper mâché structures, some covered in a thin layer of enamel, others plain as plain could be. One, a jade-like vase with a long and slender neck, gurgled softly, as if it contained a river. Zhi Wenku recognized it immediately as the Moon Jade Jar, a device created to draw back the floods that'd nearly drowned a kingdom. Or, surely, a copy.

No surprise the puppet handed the jar to Zhi Wenku. A complete surprise when she realized it was the real thing. She stared at it, feeling the cool jade beneath her fingers and the power it contained. At her expression, Count Li said, "I believe Kang Huang captured it when he took over this kingdom. He must have given it to Pan Wei to study."

Zhi Wenku had no doubt Pan Wei's copy, if copy had ever been made, would be a capable piece of work. The original was far better. She was about to have the puppet lead them outside when she noticed a glass jar full of a peculiar sort of liquid, one that changed colors constantly. "Count Li... is that?"

The Count looked at the jar. Swore in his brother's voice. "Five-element ink. I should have forced my way in here years ago!" he snapped. "That damned stuff is why we're in this fix in the first place."

They didn't have time to discuss it. Zhi Wenku gestured to the puppet. "Lock up tight and lead us outside by a back exit, please."

Within minutes they were outside and none too soon. Zhi Wenku gazed at the hillside, watching flames rise towards twilit skies, clouds of smoke glowing above them. Not much time. Not much time at all.

"Pang Hua, can you fly and use that umbrella to spread what your brother's parasol consumes at the same time?" At his agreement and obvious understanding, she gestured for him to be off.

Count Li inverted his parasol. "I'm ready when you are."

Removing the jar's stopper, Zhi Wenku set the long contained flood waters free.

弟子

The skies to the east were just lightening when Qing and Xinglu headed out of the city towards a much brighter light to the northwest. As the Emperor had warned, a mountain burned brilliantly, its southern side ablaze.

Qing drew his *qi* together, focusing it on the air, hoping to bring down another storm. Not damp enough. Not nearly damp enough. He'd used water from the river the other day, but while there were streams, there were no rivers close enough here.

"Can you eat some of that?"

"Gods," Xinglu muttered. "I can, but I haven't rebalanced my foundations after my last tribulation yet."

Qing understood. Cultivation was a tricky process, requiring a cultivator to push themselves past their current limits. Xinglu had done so through his tribulation earlier, but that wasn't all he had to do. Before he could take in more power, he needed to balance what he had or risk *qi* deviation.

"Help me look for water."

"Right."

They flew closer. Flew above the mountains north of Chang'an's river plain. Lit mostly by the fire, all Qing could see was smoke and flames. All he could smell was burning wood. If there was water sufficient for him to use, it was too well hidden for him to find.

Xinglu sniffed the air sharply, broad nostrils spread wide as his entire attention was drawn off to his left. He whined in his throat, an excited hound on the hunt and Qing knew he must have scented something. Must have scented water.

Following his friend's guidance, Qing turned his attention in that direction. As a former koi, he'd ordinarily have no trouble finding any water nearby. But the fire interfered, confusing his senses, making it nearly impossible to spot what Xinglu had found.

He pushed closer, risking the heat of the flames, choking on smoke, wondering if he'd a hope of doing anything at his current strength and competence. Then he felt a thick stream, cold and stagnant and lifeless, pouring down from somewhere amid the smoke.

Though he couldn't understand why that water was devoid of life, Qing didn't waste time contemplating it. Water was water and he didn't need it to be fresh to transform it to a storm. He caught hold of the liquid with his *qi*, spreading it out into the air and using the surrounding smoke to form clouds.

"HEY!" The voice was Pang Hua's, and a moment later the man rose towards them, spinning wildly in the air as he aimed his inverted umbrella towards the ground, a thick stream of water pouring out rapidly. He looked furious, but when he spotted them, he calmed down immediately. "Oh. It's you two. Right. Are you up to the job, dragonling?"

Qing had no idea where the water jetting from Pang Hua's umbrella came from and he didn't care. "Yes," he said, with far more confidence than he felt. He grew to his largest form, knowing he needed to use all the *qi* he could draw on for this. "I'm going to have to be."

Clouds gathered above them, dark as the smoke below, glowing faintly from the fire's light. Lightning flashed. Flashed again. All while Qing drove the water Pang Hua fed him up and up and up, chilling it, condensing it into clouds, until at last, too heavy to hold on, they loosed their contents onto the mountain below.

Steam rose. So did more flames, but only in one area, where a small and long since abandoned village stood. Qing intensified his efforts, dousing the fire among the trees, then focused his attention on the only source of flames left. He flew closer, spotting a small child-like figure standing in the center of that village, screaming and waving a fan far too big for her.

The fan was clearly another copy, probably of the Five Flame Seven Plume Fan. If so, it was yet another device not quite as powerful as the original. Its flames would have turned everything to ash by now, otherwise. Qing focused his rain on the girl and her weapon. Everything else was damped down but she had to be stopped before she escaped and set everything off again elsewhere.

The child screamed, her voice echoing through the mountains, like the caws of a gigantic flock of crows. "NOT AGAIN. NOT AGAIN! I'LL BURN YOU ALL! I SWEAR I'LL BURN YOU ALL!"

Something flew at Qing, a small pagoda, spinning in the air and headed straight for him. Except Pang Hua intercepted the thing before it reached him, grasping it tight in one hand. "Keep at it, dragonling. You're doing fine!"

Encouraged, knowing he wasn't dealing with a mere mortal child, Qing tightened his storm, drawing the lightning together into a single bolt. Then he released it on the fan wielder, blasting the weapon from her grasp and straight past Xinglu.

As his friend snatched the fan from the air, Qing called out, "Destroy the maker's mark." At the same time he turned towards the infuriated 'child', intending to catch her in his claws so she could do no more harm. Except she pulled a talisman—a teleportation talisman—from her ragged leather clothing and released its energy.

Qing dived after her, trying to stop her a moment too late. The child disappeared, leaving him skidding against the ground and slamming into a large stone door set into the mountainside. Stunned, he lay still and tried to catch his breath, hoping his Master wouldn't be too annoyed with him for letting the enemy escape.

CHAPTER 11
A Meeting of Minds

"**H**onestly, child...."
        "I'm sorry!"

"...*yang* rich root, simmered in a pot until soft..."
"It smells delicious."
"For a demon hound, you have interesting tastes, Young Xinglu."

Ignoring the others, Zhi Wenku gazed at her apprentice, torn between an urge to shake him and an urge to drag him into a tight embrace. What was wrong with his foolish head that he truly thought she'd be more upset by the enemy's escape over his safety?

"...the hottest of spices from the southern lands..."
"Oof. That hurts!"
"Count, who told you to taste it?"

For that matter, did Qing even realize what he looked like right now? Turned human, his clothes were in good order, but he'd scraped himself up badly chasing that child/not-child down. His right cheek was raw and bloodied, his left wrist so badly twisted she feared he'd broken it. Gods knew what his belly and lower body looked like, but it couldn't be good.

"...glutinous rice, cooked tender..."
"I thought you were an alchemist, not a cook."
"There isn't much difference, sometimes."

Seeing Qing about to apologize again, Zhi Wenku tapped his thick skull with her fan and said, "You can't be blamed for failing to catch her. You couldn't have foreseen her having a teleportation talisman and you certainly couldn't have moved fast enough to stop her escape."

"Fat from a wild boar... Xinglu, if you dare eat that raw..."
"Sorry Master."
"OW!"
"That goes for you, too, Pang Hua!"

Tired of the interruptions, Zhi Wenku looked dourly on the others, where they hovered over the cauldron where Shen Wei was preparing medicine—or was it dinner?—for Pan Wei's damaged *hun* soul. They noticed her reaction and immediately stopped talking so loud. Not that she expected it to last.

Turning back to her apprentice, she noted that he still looked unconvinced, huge dark eyes damp with unshed tears. The child did take his failures to heart so. "Enough," she murmured. "You did well, helping to stop the fire. Did you have to use all your *qi* again?"

"I controlled it better this time. I could probably make another small storm if I have the water to work with.... uhm... Master, what was that water anyway? It was really old."

The long contained waters from a centuries-past flood would certainly be old and stale. "We'll talk about that later. I don't think it's important. Unless you think it's harmful?"

Qing's brows drew together tightly as he considered the possibilities. "I wouldn't want to dump it directly on a field, or in a river. It might shock the plants or the fish. But it wouldn't do much damage aside from that."

"Good. I'll trust your expertise on that. Now let me take care of your injuries. We have to wait until Shen Wei is finished, anyway."

By the time Qing was bandaged, Shen Wei had filled a bowl with something that looked a bit like congee, given congee wasn't bright red and orange and didn't bubble like lava. "Are you sure about that?" she couldn't help asking.

"I don't have the right materials for making a proper *Yang* restorative potion." Shen Wei set the bowl in front of Pan Wei's *hun* soul. "Go ahead. It's hot, so be warned."

Pan Wei took the spoon, almost dropping it several times as his *hun* body fizzled and faded. Then he managed to get a small bite into his mouth and his expression lit up. "Oh yes!" Without hesitation, he set to downing the stuff, apparently immune to the effects of all the various spices Shen Wei had included.

By the time he'd finished, his entire body seemed a great deal more solid. Still translucent, but no longer bent over from exhaustion, no longer fading and faltering every few minutes. He sat back. Sighed. Then looked up at them all, "So much better. So good. Thank you!" A puzzled expression crossed his face. "Except... could I ask how you got in? I don't see my disciples with you at all and strangers aren't supposed to be inside my craft hall. Especially now I'm dead."

"Disciples?" Xinglu repeated. "I thought you only had the two and Da...."

Before he could finish the sentence, Shen Wei set his folded fan in front of his apprentice's mouth. "Don't use her name."

"Eh? Why shouldn't he use Da Ping's name?" the *hun* soul asked curiously.

Remembering how the part of Pan Wei in the scroll had referred to Da Ping and Pingping, Zhi Wenku realized this was another way to work around the poor man's trauma. "It's rude for an apprentice to be calling a Master by a nickname like that, that's all."

"Oh. Yes. I forget Da Ping's a Master now... I've been forgetting a great deal, I realize." Looking troubled, Pan Wei gazed around worriedly, hand going towards his throat as if he almost remembered his death.

Zhi Wenku said carefully, "We need to discuss a great deal and not just amongst ourselves. Master Pan, can you leave this place and come back to the Soul Protection Society with us?"

A flick of the hand beckoned the umbrella puppet over. A single step melded Pan Wei's spirit into its substance. A papery voice spoke, "When I died, my *po* soul seems to have attached itself to my works. I can't cultivate or create, but I can join you through this piece."

That was good, Zhi Wenku thought. Because they needed this part of Pan Wei's input into the situation. What they didn't need was for anyone else to get into this stronghold.

Not when the man's treasury contained the thing she was certain the one behind all this nonsense wanted: the Five Element Ink. The very thing that'd given Daoping the power to change her world for herself. Speaking of which, "Before we leave, I want you to lock your vault and protect it with every trap you have."

Because the last thing they needed was for their enemy to repeat Daoping's sins.

弟子

If Qing weren't a dragon, and stronger than humans, he'd have crawled into a bunk and slept for a week or so. He was still tired enough to take his smallest dragonling form and let Master Zhi carry him like a puppy, much to everyone's obvious amusement.

He was only dimly aware of their flight back to Chang'an and Soul Protection Society's headquarters. He noticed the sunrise, but shoved his head down into the crook of Master Zhi's arm to avoid the light. The feel of the wind on his back was comfortably cool and damp, so he was almost asleep by the time they landed.

The fuss from Count Li's people roused Qing enough to lift his head and glare sleepily at all the Masters and Seniors surrounding their Chief Cultivator. "Can't they be quieter?" he demanded.

"They never are," Pan Wei's puppet said as he stepped down from behind Master Zhi. "I don't remember much but I do remember that."

"Time to wake up, little one." Master Zhi skritched Qing's head lightly, then set him on the ground to turn human. "We need everyone as alert as possible while we work out just what we know."

"We'll just go wait in the meeting room," Pang Hua said. "It'll take a while to get all these personalities settled and I want a drink."

They followed him into the main building, back to the same large room where Qing had fought the Shroud of Nine Fiery Dragons. Reminded of that situation, he suggested, "We should see if they got any information from Eunuch Zhao."

At Master Zhi's querying expression, Qing realized he hadn't told her anything about what he and Xinglu had dealt with. Embarrassed, knowing he ought to have done so already, he quickly explained what'd happened, finishing with, "The Emperor had Eunuch Zhao taken to the dungeons under Eunuch Kang's control."

"Which puts him in the Kirin Guards' hands," Pang Hua added. "Best send for Captain Li and those two nuisances. Not to mention Zhan Ping. She still has Pan Wei's scroll and I think we should get it and this one back together."

"My scroll?" Pan Wei asked.

"You'll see in a bit, boy." Pang Hua flung himself into the one of the chairs, sprawling with his feet on the table. "Xinglu, you fetch the Captain. Qing, how about you go after Zhan Ping?"

With their masters' permission, both Qing and Xinglu headed off, though it only took Qing a few minutes to persuade Master Zhan to join them. Telling her they'd found something belonging to Pan Wei proved incredibly effective, causing her to hurry ahead of him and rush into the meeting hall at top speed.

It took almost half an hour for her and Pan Wei's puppet self to stop crying over each other. She'd reacted just as strongly when she'd met the scroll protecting part of her Master's *hun* soul, but that part of Pan Wei's Self contained the man's intellect. It felt things in a very distant sort of way.

The *hun* soul in Pan Wei's puppet, on the other hand, contained the man's emotions. The pair clung to each other so tightly Qing wondered how Zhan Ping was managing to breathe.

Luckily, by the time Xinglu returned with Captain Li and his two constant companions, Master Zhan and what was left of her former Master had finally stopped crying and generally mourning the years they'd been parted. They even took note of their surroundings; the scroll opened wide so it could 'see' the whole room, while the puppet sat beside Master Zhan, spinning its umbrella around on the tip of its finger.

"Is that supposed to be you, uncle?" Li Aiqing asked, glancing behind him. Count Li had finally shaken off his Society responsibilities onto others so he could join them.

"I believe so, Ah-Qing." Count Li scanned the room thoughtfully. "Do we have everyone we need?"

It was Master Zhi who answered sardonically. "Do you think Eunuch Kang should attend as well? Or perhaps the Empress?"

A sudden bark of laughter escaped Kang Qiyun's lips. "She's just a baby," he scoffed.

That made everyone look at him and he seemed to realize he'd overstepped his bounds. More politely, he said, "I mean, Her Imperial Majesty is only fourteen and inexperienced. Best not put herself in danger again for no reason."

Count Li chuckled. "Some young people should learn to keep thoughts to themselves better, especially if they want their shins unbruised." He gestured for the embarrassed man and his companions to find a seat and for some reason turned to Qing. "Do you have any other guests to suggest? Or suggestions, for that matter?"

Though he knew he was being teased, Qing took the question seriously. Short of finding Pan Wei's third *hun* soul—a likely impossibility—everyone directly involved in the situation seemed to be there. They could bring Commander Pan or Eunuch Kang Zi in as well, but Qing had a feeling that'd be too much. Innocently, teasing back, Qing asked, "The Emperor?"

As everyone else laughed, Master Zhi squeezed the bridge of her nose with her fingers, her fan showing the image of a familiar pond, a small fish being thrown back into it. He grinned saucily at her, knowing perfectly well she was amused, and added, "My only suggestion is accounting for all the pieces of... that woman's... work that we've found or encountered so far."

Master Zhi agreed, pulling a writing kit from her sleeve and handing it to him, her expectations clear. After all, if he was going to suggest secretarial work, he should be prepared to be the secretary. Without complaint, because he'd expected it, Qing laid out a blank scroll, took up his brush and ink, and waited expectantly.

弟子

Before they could discuss Daoping's works, they had to discuss Daoping, and that meant making sure Pan Wei's *hun* souls could handle hearing her name. They didn't need the pair to lose their self-control in the middle of their war council.

Zhi Wenku turned to the puppet, mildly amused that he'd set his feet on the table in a pose precisely like Pang Hua's. "This won't be an easy discussion for you. Are you strong enough to handle being reminded of how you died?"

"How can you say it so rudely?" Zhan Ping demanded, automatically defending what was left of her master.

The scroll showed the words, [[She's right, Da Ping. We don't want that part of me getting so upset we can't talk.]] It twisted in the air, clearly thinking about the matter. [[Call her Pingping. That'll help.]]

The nickname was embarrassing, but Zhi Wenku accepted the inevitable. "Then do you recall all the items Pingping created when she was your disciple?"

More thoughtful twisting. [[I set both her and Da Ping the task of trying to improve on my own creations. But anything Pingping made that actually worked went straight to her father. Quite a few, really. She wasn't as good as Da Ping, but she was capable.]]

"Until she added fire to the mix. I told her leather and wood wouldn't mix well with it but she didn't want to listen."

"She wanted to be like her father," the puppet added mournfully. "He used fire too. And she was doing so well with living plants."

"That would explain why—aside from the puppets—practically every one of her creations we've fought have involved fire. Not the pagoda, but...."

"Oh, the pagoda has fire in it, too. Between the inner and outer walls." Pang Hua pulled the thing from his sleeve, shaking it so hard it seemed to whimper in his grasp. "Don't fuss, brat. I can still take out your mark if you'd prefer."

"THE SCROLL FLEW OVER QING'S HEAD."

As the pagoda fell silent, Zhi Wenku coughed and asked, "Did the puppets that attacked last night also have fire involved?"

"It's possible. I'll have someone look into it." Count Li wrote a few words in the air that drifted off to whomever he'd delegated the task to. "In the meantime, shall we take your apprentice's advice and list the items Pingping left us?"

Considering that a good idea, Zhi Wenku counted on her fingers. "So far we've encountered a copy each of the Pot of Ten Thousand Crows, the Five Flames and Seven Plumes Fan, the Exquisite Pagoda, the Nine Fiery Dragons Shroud, and the World Umbrella. That last appears to have been broken as I've yet to see it in operation."

"There's the Flaming Belt Sword as well, Master. I ruined its mark just before Xinglu and I went to Fenghua Shan." Qing finished writing everything down, adding, "The fan and the sword's maker's mark were destroyed. They may not be a risk anymore. Unless repairing the mark would repair them as well?"

[[It could, if its creator was powerful enough. Pingping wasn't that good.]] The scroll flew over Qing's head to examine the list. [[Six items, so she didn't put her *hun* soul into them. You can't split that into more than three parts.]]

"There's also that little girl," Xinglu pointed out. "She obviously wasn't a mortal being. Couldn't possibly be an artifact, and she didn't look like a puppet."

That made Pan Wei's puppet laugh. "She could so be an artifact if she was old enough and absorbed enough *qi*. Truly powerful artifacts can cultivate a human form."

Zhi Wenku already knew that much and she said so. "I didn't see her before she escaped but I did hear her screaming and it sounded a great deal like crows. Could Pingping's copy of the Pot of Ten Thousand Crows be that strong?" She'd been thinking on that, and on the pagoda in Pang Hua's hands, for a bit now. "Or did she create a puppet to carry her *hun* soul after she died?"

"Even if it was that strong, there's still a problem," Pang Hua countered. "Even if her better creations acquired awareness, it takes time for an artifact to cultivate a human form."

A thought occurred to Zhi Wenku. "What about her *po* soul? Perhaps those parts survived because she split it as well?"

Qing counted the lines on his notes. "But Master, a *po* soul separates into seven identities. We've only come across six."

Gently, because she knew he was tired and not thinking clearly, she told him, "The seventh might still be out there, hiding and waiting for its chance."

They all took the idea in and Captain Li said quietly, "That may be true." When they looked at him, he continued, "The Emperor wanted me to tell you what we've discovered, but I didn't like to interrupt."

"And?"

"Eunuch Zhao was very forthcoming about the part he played in this matter." Captain Li took out a small notebook, going over it quickly. "Firstly, he came across a scroll in the records house while trying to find evidence regarding Eunuch Kang's family."

When they all looked at Kang Qiyun, the young man flushed. "Kang bro's not literally my brother," he said quickly. "He just helped take care of me when I was little. I don't have anything to do with his family's politics."

"You always say that when he looks like he might be in trouble," Li Aiqing grumbled.

"But it's true!"

A sigh from Captain Li. "Shut up, you two." When the pair fell silent, he continued, "The scroll in question was written in strange ink that changed colors. He learned that Dao... that Pingping... hid a powerful treasure in her father's vault. One of several that could ensure her return, if they were all brought together. We searched for the scroll but it's gone missing."

That fit with the Empress' and Eunuch Kang's story. Zhi Wenku was about to say as much but she noted a guilty expression cross Qing's face. Knowing her apprentice, she gazed at him levelly, waiting until he reached into his sleeve and pulled out a scroll. "I think that's because I took it, Master," he said meekly. "I meant to show you but we kept getting distracted."

Completely offended, Kang Qiyun demanded, "You took that from the Records Office? You're not supposed to just take things from the Records Office! That's practically criminal!"

Before the young man could really get going, Count Li said gently, "It's a good thing he did, don't you think? Consider what might have happened if Eunuch Zhao got worried about our investigation and hid it. This isn't the time to concern yourself with Imperial rights. Especially given all the secrets the Emperor and his wife have been keeping from me?"

As Kang Qiyun wilted, the Count took the scroll from Qing, carefully removing the uppermost layer and spreading the thing out between them all. Despairingly, he muttered, "I destroyed her brush. I destroyed her ink. I tried to destroy every piece of writing she left using that damned brush of hers. I should have known she'd planned for it."

It appeared Eunuch Zhao had discovered the hidden writing and hidden it again once he'd learned what Daoping had left behind. They'd been right to think each artifact contained a seventh of the woman's *po* soul, with this scroll describing the process needed to restore her to life. Six of the artifacts were the ones already encountered. The last was the Master of Puppets, an artifact Zhi Wenku had never known of before Count Li'd mentioned it.

She pointed to the name. "This was hidden in the Emperor's personal vault. Could it have been what attacked His Majesty?"

Rubbing his arm nervously, Kang Qiyun offered, "It looked more like a *jiangshi* to me."

A scoff from Li Aiqing. "We barely saw it, it moved so fast. How can you be sure of anything, given you were...."

Captain Li growled at his brother, "Be quiet." He turned his attention to Zhi Wenku. "I saw it as well. It resembled a corpse, yes, but now I think of it, it could have been a puppet covered in leather. Whatever it was, we were too busy keeping the Emperor alive to chase it."

Zhi Wenku understood the priority. "No fault to any of you on that." She turned her attention back to the scroll. "This mentions needing something vital to the task in Master Pan's craft.... workshop. I'm certain I know what that thing was and just how dangerous it'd be for the enemy to get at it."

"True," Shen Wei added his thoughts for the first time that morning. "But it might also be useful bait, if we can persuade them to bite."

Zhi Wenku didn't like the idea much. She didn't want that ink in anyone's hands, ever again. And yet she had to admit Shen Wei was right. They needed to draw the enemy out and they needed to capture every last remaining piece. Preferably before they set the whole country alight.

弟子

Lacking a better choice, they all agreed that a trap must be set. They also agreed that they didn't dare use the actual Five-Colored ink for bait. It was Qing who suggested, "Would the Emperor send his people to Fenghua Shan to examine the situation? Someone could claim to have found a cache of the ink in the ruins."

"What about the brush, though?" Xinglu countered. "The ink on its own isn't much use."

"Master Pan, did you have a copy of the brush that you made?"

"I don't remember." [[Of course. How do you think I got in here?]]

The simultaneous answers weren't surprising. Pan Wei's *hun* soul of emotion wouldn't maintain much in the way of memory. And the *hun* soul of intellect hadn't really explained how he'd wound up inside that scroll. For that matter, "The Empress said you made the Emperor a new arm. How did you manage that?"

Quite suddenly the scroll displayed an image of a huge room full of an artificer's tools. Paper rabbits browsed around on the floor, paper bats flew overhead around a slim dark-clad figure, so similar in shape and form to the puppet sitting beside Master Zhan that it was obvious who it was. The figure waved gleefully, then the image faded and words formed once more. [[It's a lucky thing I was experimenting with the way Book Hunters' Warehouses work. I'd never have created the whole thing in the time I had before I was beheaded.]]

Master Zhi sighed. "That's a distraction," she pointed out. "The important question is the Five Color Brush. Did your master have the original?"

[[I don't believe so. That one disappeared centuries ago. Most of our artifices were designed based on what they were supposed to do. I've no idea if they were anywhere near as capable.]]

There was no doubt in Qing's mind that Pan Wei's creations had been remarkable. He might even have said so but the main point was the brush. "Where did your copy go, then?"

[[Oh, in here with me. I don't have any ink though. Used up the dish I worked with creating this scroll and protecting my workshop.]]

The rest of the ink, as already determined, was hidden in the depths of Pan Wei's vault, as secure as it could be. But, "If someone got hold of one, could they create more ink and use it?"

[[They'd have to know the recipe. Which, if Pingping is involved, might be possible, given her father gave it to her. He never actually told me. Didn't trust me that much, towards the end.]]

The puppet said quietly, "He didn't trust anyone much towards the end."

Quite suddenly Kang Qiyun yawned, then went wide-eyed with worry. "Er, sorry. It's not that you're boring. It's just...."

Actually, he was right. They kept getting distracted from the main point. Qing looked at his master and wasn't surprised when she said, "Right, you three go back to the palace and make sure the Emperor sends men to investigate the ruins on Fenghua Shan. They're to send people back with the fake ink and bring it to... Count Li, where's a good place?"

"My pavilion. I can trap anyone who tries to steal it there."

The pavilion was where Xinglu had undergone his tribulation and the array embedded in the stone platform could, indeed, be used as a trap. Qing certainly wouldn't have attempted to break past its magically created walls.

"We should have more ready than just the array," Pang Hua noted. "We'll add some extra protection around the place."

"Mm. Agreed." Count Li turned his attention to Master Zhi. "You and Shen Wei should go up with the Emperor's people and bring the fake ink to us."

"Agreed."

"Young Qing, Xinglu, if your masters don't object, you two come with us.

Pang Hua and I will guard two of the points on the array. You can help bolster the other two."

Seeing their masters agreed, Qing asked, "What about Master Zhan and Masters Pan?" He indicated the three across from him. "They don't have enough cultivation to help fight."

"They should stay safely in our guest quarters." At Master Zhan's clear relief, Count Li added, "They need to rest, anyway."

Pan Wei's puppet looked slightly dejected. "I wish I could be more use."

"As do I, child. You're both too damaged at the moment. Use the time wisely and perhaps that will change."

A soft voice interrupted their discussion. "Uhm...." When they all looked at Li Aiqing, he blushed bright pink at the attention. "Uncle, is there a reason why the Emperor wouldn't confiscate the ink for himself?"

That made Kang Qiyun glare at him. "Oh, of course. Because the Emperor is foolish enough to have something like that brought into his palace." A toss of the hands. "There's ignorant and there's outright stupid."

Count Li sighed. "There's also far too talkative for one's own good, child. Don't keep interrupting." As Kang Qiyun flushed and fell silent again, the Count continued, "Or at least time your speech better, when it's actually useful."

"Yes, sir. Sorry sir."

A thought occurred to Qing. "I'm sure anyone who knows what we're supposed to have found will believe the ink's being taken for examination. But would most soldiers tell just anyone about the matter?"

Kang Qiyun looked at Qing, clearly sensing where he was going with the idea. "Now wait!" he protested, only to be shushed by Captain Li.

Qing ignored the pair. "So maybe we need to have someone people expect to talk about things they aren't supposed to talk about it in places where anyone could hear? It might draw in a few uninvolved thieves, but Pingping, or whomever it is causing trouble, would hear of it too."

"And who, pray tell, are you suggesting mouth off that way?" Kang Qiyun demanded. When they all gazed levelly at him, though, he couldn't maintain the pretense and folded his arms across his chest and pouted. "Oh, of course. Use the poor orphaned boy as a messenger. I don't mind."

"That's good," Captain Li said firmly, setting his hand on Kang Qiyun's shoulder while Li Aiqing patted the other. "Because they're right. When it comes to spreading baseless rumor and confusing the issue, you're a past master of the skill."

Looking like he'd rather tell his two companions to 'scram', Kang Qiyun turned a resigned look on Count Li and sighed. "Yes. Of course. I'll do it. It's not like I have anything else important to be doing right now."

That decided, they all set off in their appointed directions to their appointed duties.

CHAPTER 12
The Best Laid Plans

It took hours to implement their plan. The Emperor sent his men up to Fenghua Shan with Zhi Wenku and Shen Wei. Commander Fan pretended to find the jar of ink and—after a brief argument—allowed them to take the ceramic jar back to Count Li's pavilion. By the time they were flying across Chang'an's river valley towards Count Li's mansion it was well past noon.

All through this, Zhi Wenku couldn't help feeling like she'd forgotten something important. When she said so, Shen Wei admitted, "I feel the same. The trouble is, there's so much going on and so many different secrets being kept that I can't tell what fits where. Or, indeed, if they fit together at all."

Thinking about it, there really were far too many pieces involved. This might be a good time to account for two of them, just to be sure. "Count Li and his brother aren't human, are they?"

"Now that much is certain. He's never actually told anyone what they are, though I wouldn't be surprised if they were some small Gods."

Quite possibly true. Except the Count and Pang Hua's reaction to that broken copy of the World Umbrella felt terribly significant. At first, Zhi Wenku had thought he might be a servant of the World Umbrella's master, Guang Mu, but the way the brothers spoke and behaved, along with the nature of their powers, suggested something more.

They were alone, making Zhi Wenku's next question safe to ask without far too interested ears attending. "Could they be an artifact? The World Umbrella itself?"

Shen Wei turned a startled look on her and nearly lost control of his sword. Once he recovered, he fanned himself sharply, embarrassed flowers flushing pink on his fan's surface. Then, "I never even considered that. I'm not a religious man, I'm afraid. I don't have every God or Godly artifact memorized the way you do."

It was Zhi Wenku's Chief Cultivator who knew all the Gods, from first to last, both born and unborn, lost and restored. Zhi Wenku's lore didn't extend nearly that far. "It just makes sense. They're clearly one being, separated because even at half-power their strength is far beyond mortal. And my records say the World Umbrella connects reality and chaos."

"Both of which fit our Chief Cultivator and his brother all too well." Shen

Wei considered that. "Do you think it has anything to do with the situation?"

"He engineered Kang Huang's fall and stopped Daoping when she followed in her father's footsteps, so perhaps?" A thought occurred to Zhi Wenku, "There's that boy, Kang Qiyun, too. He's supposed to be Kang Huang's descendant, and there's definitely something odd about him."

"Mm. Yes. Though he's always been a bit odd; always getting into trouble with Li Aiqing and always getting dragged out of scrapes by Captain Li. Count Li doesn't seem worried, though, so perhaps he isn't a problem?"

Oh, that boy was obviously a problem. Whether he was the problem at the heart of this mess, however, was something yet to be determined. They'd have to keep an eye on him.

Seeing they were almost to the pavilion, seeing the Count, his brother and their apprentices waiting for them, Zhi Wenku set that thought aside, landing beside the Count and holding up their bait. The pale blue ceramic gleamed in the sunlight, its surface covered in protective arrays.

"Any difficulties?" Count Li asked, and a worried expression crossed his face when Zhi Wenku told him 'no'. "Not even a sign of interference or spies?"

To be honest, Zhi Wenku understood Count Li's concern. To be honest, she felt it too. To be honest, she was borrowing trouble. Except there were times and places where she couldn't trust a situation to stay calm. There'd been far too many attacks from unexpected directions.

Still, all they could do at the moment was wait and see. "By now those boys will have gossiped to anyone who'd listen about what we 'found' up on Fenghua Shan," she said. "It's mid-afternoon. If our enemy takes the bait they'll be here soon." She took the jar to the center of the pavilion and set it down.

"True," Count Li agreed, indicating a door standing alone among the rocks. "You two wait in my side-space while the boys and I set the trap."

The side-space in question resembled Count Li's guest room. Indeed, Zhi Wenku thought it might actually be that place, despite the windows showing the same view as the mountain they'd been on. There were snacks on the table and plenty of books to read, although neither Zhi Wenku nor Shen Wei wanted a distraction.

It only took a few minutes for Count Li and his companions to finish the work and when they came into the side-space, both Qing and Xinglu had the proud look of children allowed to take part in adult matters. They'd likely learned a few things, helping set the trap.

"Now we wait," Pang Hua grumbled. "I hate waiting."

Zhi Wenku didn't blame him, though she could sit for hours, or days, simply meditating. "It doesn't help that we don't know anything about the enemy and thus have no idea of how intelligent or capable they actually are."

"Can't be terribly bright, given all they do is throw fire at us."

Although Pang Hua was right in that much, Zhi Wenku felt they'd be wrong to underestimate the enemy for that one reason. "We'll wait until morning," she suggested. "Then see."

"Still don't like it, but yes. Until morning."

It was only hour before something happened. The trouble was, what happened wasn't a fiery attempt to claim that jar of 'ink', or any sort of attack at all. Rather, the interruption came from Chang'an yet again, as a flare went off from the north-western corner of the city. From, in fact, the center of the Society's headquarters. Count Li rose to his feet, glaring through the window at Chang'an, expression icy cold.

Without waiting for anyone's opinion, he wrote in the air, setting their little side-space spinning as it relocated itself. As he and his brother leapt out the window to find out what was wrong, Zhi Wenku glanced at her companions. Shrugged. Then followed the same path without a moment's hesitation.

弟子

Qing's master almost never rushed into trouble without checking what lay ahead. The fact that she did so now told Qing just how perilous the situation was. He flew after her in dragonling form, using every sense he had to search for danger.

He found nothing. Just the basic *qi* energy emitted from the Soul Protection Society's arrays and formations. Was the signal a trick? Had they rushed back and left the supposed jar of ink unprotected? It wouldn't matter much—the ink wasn't real—yet it'd mean they'd lost track of their unknown enemy yet again.

A crowd of Society guards surrounded Count Li and Pang Hua, talking fast and pointing towards the entrance to the guest housing. Pan Wei's scroll spun around them agitatedly, the words written on its surface appearing and disappearing too fast to read.

Catching up to the others, Qing listened intently to the guards' explanations. "...don't know. That scroll just came out and started bashing us, like it wanted us to do something. Then it shot that firework."

So Pan Wei was the one who'd signaled? Qing should have realized the Soul Protection Society wouldn't use a firework to signal for help. They'd have something much more attention getting.

It was obvious they'd get no sense from Pan Wei until he calmed down. Qing hurried after the scroll, the only one who could follow its intricate patterns and outfly it. No easy task, even for him, so wildly did the thing fling itself around in the effort to make its point known.

"Stop that, Master Pan!" he said, once he grasped hold of the thing. "Calm down enough to tell us what's wrong?"

It took several tense minutes but the scroll finally went still enough for Pan Wei to write, [[She's taken Da Ping and my other self!]]

"She?" Count Li repeated. "She, who?"

[[Pingping! Daoping! That rotten brat disciple who I should never have taught a single damned thing!]]

"She walked right in and just took them? How?"

[[Not walked in. She was in that scroll of hers the way I'm in here! Only it's all her *hun* soul. I couldn't fight her. I was just lucky she didn't realize I was here!]]

Rapidly changing images flowed across the scroll as Pan Wei showed them what'd happened. Pan Wei's puppet and Master Zhan sitting beside the pond, talking. Pan Wei's scroll leaning against a wall, watching them and listening. The sudden arrival of Senior Yao, carrying the scroll Qing had borrowed—no, stolen—from the records room. Seeming dazed, Senior Yao had offered the scroll to Master Zhan, only for the damned thing to leap from his hands and wrap itself around both Master Zhan and the puppet.

Pan Wei's scroll had sent his rabbit army to attack Senior Yao but the scroll had set fire to them. By the time Pan Wei had saved his pets, Senior Yao, the scroll, and the two captives were gone.

Count Li frowned. "Yao Deng is a close-minded, righteous, overly-ambitious ass. But he isn't a traitor."

"I agree," Master Shen offered. "But he may be controlled."

A thought occurred to Qing. "Can you trace him? Xinglu mentioned something about your tokens once." He pointed to the jade piece hanging from Master Shen's belt.

The look of approval Master Zhi gave Qing made him feel warm inside. "Well thought of, apprentice." She considered the matter. Glanced inquiringly at Count Li. When the man nodded, she continued, "You and Xinglu go check the tracker. Send word if it looks like he's with Daoping. We'll search here for clues."

Oh, being trusted to work alone was recognition indeed. Qing took his human form, shared an eager grin with his best friend and followed Xinglu through the main building to a large room with a huge map across the floor. "This is nice."

Xinglu puffed up proudly. "I helped draw this version," he told Qing. "It's nothing compared to what your sect can do, I'm sure."

"We just have a globe and it isn't complete." Qing didn't mention their ability to focus down to specific places. He didn't want to brag. "This is more than enough." He scanned the map, determining that it covered everything from the eastern coast to the western desert, with Chang'an sitting in the northwest on a flat river plain between two mountainous regions. North were dry valleys and desert. South were mountains and more mountains.

Xinglu went to the far wall and opened the cabinet containing row upon row of jade tokens, each marked with a name. Taking Senior Yao's, Xinglu set it in an indentation in the wall, where it sent a beam of light towards the map. Qing frowned, kneeling beside the place where the light struck. "This says he's still inside Society headquarters."

"Maybe it's just his jade token? We're supposed to keep it with us at all times, but...."

But, obviously, it could be left somewhere; forgotten or deliberately abandoned. "Should we check?"

"Mm. Best." Xinglu took the token from the indentation and inserted it into a compass he'd pulled from his *qiankun* sleeve. "This way. It's pointing towards the healer's hall."

The Society's healer's hall was in a plain white building towards the western side of the grounds. Unlike the alchemical hall or the mechanist hall, the building didn't need reinforcement, so the walls and roof were simple as simple could be. Inside, everything was ruthlessly clean and polished, sign that the Master of this division had firm opinions about sanitation. Everything was calm and beautiful, but Qing couldn't help feeling like something was terribly wrong.

"I smell blood," Xinglu said suddenly. "Human blood."

Qing did too, though he wasn't connoisseur enough to know what species. They followed the scent, neither surprised to see the compass guiding them to the same place. And, when they broke open the door to a storage room, they weren't at all shocked to find Senior Yao bleeding on the floor from a blow to the skull, moaning softly.

Xinglu rushed off to fetch the healers, while Qing used what skills he had to make sure the man stayed alive.

弟子

Zhi Wenku's lips were tight as she watched Master Healer Mu finish bandaging Senior Yao. The man was lucky to be alive, not least because he and everyone else had been outright ordered to stay quiet inside the Society's grounds. Doubly lucky his would-be killer had been interrupted and forced to leave him where he lay.

"How was I supposed to know he'd attack me?" Senior Yao demanded weakly. "I've seen him with the palace guards before. The tall one with Captain Li."

Zhi Wenku frowned. Kang Qiyun? When she repeated the name, Count Li said quietly, "I know it wasn't him. Captain Li would never leave him unprotected. But someone could have disguised themselves."

Accepting the Count's reassurance, Zhi Wenku wondered at Senior Yao's insistence that he return the scroll right in the middle of a difficult and dangerous operation. All right, so he hadn't been told exactly what was going on, but he ought to have worked out that today was not at all the time.

Count Li clearly agreed. "Even if you felt the scroll should be returned, why would you think that child would be the one who'd retrieve it? I think you need to take a remedial course or two on the subject of mental defense."

"We all could," Zhi Wenku grumbled. "We should have realized that scroll was more than it appeared." Especially given Pan Wei's scroll for an example. "I really should have examined it more carefully."

If Pan Wei was correct—and likely he was—the scroll Qing had taken from the records hall had been more than just an attempt to change Daoping's fate. It'd contained some part of herself. Whether that part was her whole *hun* soul or just a portion didn't matter. It obviously intended to gather her broken pieces to revive herself. The question was, could she, now so many of her artifacts had been ruined?

"Tell us exactly how it happened," Zhi Wenku told the man, only to need her demand repeated by Count Li because Senior Yao wouldn't listen to an outsider. "Quickly, please."

Sulkily, Senior Yao told them, "I found the scroll in our dining hall, just sitting there. It obviously belonged to the Imperial Records, so I sent a note to the palace to send someone to come fetch it. You said we couldn't leave. You never said a word about not letting anyone in."

"That isn't even remotely true and you know it," Count Li snapped. "I said to stay put and stay quiet. Quiet should include not bringing outsiders onto our grounds in the middle of a lockdown. And I distinctly remember using the word lockdown when I gave the order."

Face full of grievance, Senior Yao muttered, "I didn't pay attention. I was busy cleaning up after everyone's mess." Seeing his Chief Cultivator was about the closest to losing his long temper as he'd ever been, Senior Yao hurriedly continued, "He came and I gave him the scroll."

"And then?"

"We were talking about... what were we talking about... oh, yes, how things were going to change with Eunuch Zhao arrested and wondering if the Emperor would really put Eunuch Kang in charge. Oh, and he asked after Master Mu. Something about wanting to see if she could prescribe something to help the Empress conceive."

That made Master Mu glare at the man as she finished her task. "Aside from that not being any man's business, except—perhaps—the Emperor's, you still haven't explained how you ended up here in my storage rooms?"

"He said he knew a prescription that'd help the Emperor father a son. I... You know, I don't know why, but I brought him here to fetch the ingredients."

Oh. Good. "You were certainly being controlled," Zhi Wenku snapped. "You don't even remember visiting the guest area with the scroll, do you?"

"Guest area? Why would I take the scroll to the guest area?"

Count Li ignored his senior disciple's indignant question and turned to Master Mu. "Can you tell if anything was taken?"

"I can, but only after a complete check. Let me take this foolish man to rest and I'll have my people investigate. From the sound of it, though, you may need to focus on other matters."

She wasn't wrong. As Master Mu had Senior Yao carried off to be cared for, Zhi Wenku turned her attention back on Count Li. "I have a theory."

"Which is?"

"I agree that that scroll Qing took contains some measure of Daoping's *hun* soul. How much and in what condition isn't clear. What is clear is that she heard us when we discussed our plans for a trap."

"That seems likely, yes."

"I don't think she was able to see, however." At everyone's curious expressions she pointed to Pan Wei's scroll, floating between Count Li and Pang Hua, staying close as if afraid of being captured. "If she could see anything in the room she would have known her Master was split between the scroll and the puppet. She only took the puppet and Zhan Ping because we never mentioned it in front of her."

Count Li considered that. "A good point. Next question, how do we find where they were taken? Pan Wei, can you track them, since your puppet is another part of yourself?"

[[If I were closer, maybe?]]

"They can't have gone far," Zhi Wenku muttered. "It's only been half an hour since Pan Wei set off that firework."

"Master?" Qing spoke softly, deferentially, in a tone that said he fully expected her to refuse. "Let me carry Master Pan's scroll and fly over the city. Maybe we'll get close enough to find the thing that way."

Qing was right to expect denial. She didn't like sending a youngster into danger. Except he wasn't a youngster anymore. He was a well trained apprentice who was becoming more and more obviously ready to take up his discipleship. In which case, "Very well. Use a concealment spell. The last thing we need is for you to be noticed."

After all, if experience had taught her anything, it was that this city was entirely too dragon-obsessed for its own good.

弟子

Hidden behind an illusion of a crow, Qing soared over the city, Pan Wei's trembling scroll held tight in his forelimbs. He couldn't blame Pan Wei for being afraid, given the danger his other *hun* soul had to be in. Yet the reaction made it obvious the division between intellect and emotion wasn't clear cut. For that matter, the *hun* soul of life must have left some part of itself in the others. How else would they be able to function at all?

Circling around, drawing lower and lower, Qing was just beginning to fear they'd find nothing when the scroll jerked in his arms. He followed its guidance northward, towards the walls of the Imperial City and past. If he'd been walking, he'd have been stopped by now. If the guards were cultivators they might still have blocked his flight. Instead he glided overhead, past government buildings, past the Emperor's palace, past courtyard after courtyard.

"This is going to annoy Master Zhi," he muttered. She and the others had stayed landbound, tracking him with his master's device. If Daoping had taken Master Zhan and Pan Wei's puppet into the Imperial City, they'd have a fine time trying to get in.

The scroll seemed to shrug, as if telling him that wasn't Pan Wei's fault. Nor was it, for all the inconvenience this would bring if they ended up alone. Qing knew better than to get too close to the enemy. He also knew how easy it was to fall into a trap, no matter how hard he might try to avoid it.

Even as he thought that, he felt the scroll tugging downwards, a strong pull that said Pan Wei's other *hun* soul must be near. Qing scanned the ground beneath him and frowned, barbels twisting and feeling and tasting the air. There was more *qi* down there, a natural source hidden below the ground, as well as arrays and formations set around that source.

He wondered how no one else had noticed the energy before now and remembered that faint flicker of natural *qi* he'd noticed days back, when he'd been chased by those fire crows. It'd faded and disappeared so quickly he'd thought it his imagination. Perhaps whomever was using it had hidden it away until now?

Unsure what to do or where to look, Qing kept moving. A palace lay below him, nearly identical to the Emperor's, as well as dozens of buildings and gardens surrounding it. Yet everything seemed too small.

"Oh. Of course. It's the Imperial Burial Grounds." That was where Eunuch Zhao had been guided by Daoping's scroll and where the Pot of Ten Thousand Crows had been hidden. Perhaps Daoping had prepared a sanctuary for herself somewhere in there as well?

Qing spotted a group of men chasing three others through the narrow pathways between the buildings. A shift in direction took him straight over the pursuit and he realized the hunters were more of Daoping's puppets.

The three being pursued were Captain Li and his two companions, Li Aiqing to the front, Captain Li in the back, both protecting Kang Qiyun from attacks that seemed to come from every direction. As for Kang Qiyun himself, he did his best to stay between his companions, blade striking out every so often when a puppet got too close. He even crushed one puppet's head between the gloved fingers of his left hand.

Qing landed on a nearby building and took his human form so he could stick Pan Wei's scroll in his sleeve and draw his whisk. Then he leapt down to the street to join the fight, breaking squash heads and crushing wooden cores as fast as he could. "Head and heart," he called out to the others. "That's the only way to break them."

"Thanks, we did notice," Li Aiqing answered, cutting off another head as he made room for Qing.

"Don't be rude, Ah-qing," Kang Qiyun gasped. "He wasn't to know we knew."

"All three of you shut up and fight," Captain Li ordered grimly. "There's too damned many of them. Where are the Palace Guards, anyway?"

"No idea. I summoned them, but I think someone's interfering." Kang Qiyun jerked back from the wall behind him as it shattered, broken open by a puppet that'd taken a more direct route to them. "We're on our own, I think." Once again he crushed the puppet's head with his left hand, then stabbed it through the wooden core.

They fought, moving forward constantly, forced towards the largest building in the burial grounds, the one built to resemble the Imperial Palace. "We're being pushed into a trap," Qing gasped.

"Another thing we noticed... I mean, yes. Sorry, Qiyun-bro. I'm just tense."

Before Kang Qiyun could respond, Captain Li reached back and swatted his younger brother. "Enough. If we're going to head into a trap, best do it with our eyes open. Apprentice Qing, please use that interesting ability of yours. I don't think the trap planned for you."

"AS HE FELL, SHIFTING AS HE WENT"

True enough. No one had mentioned him being the dragon in front of Daoping's scroll. "Right," he agreed, noting they were half-way across the courtyard in front of the fake Imperial Palace. If he were as good a cultivator as his Master or Master Shen, he might try to find out why Daoping wanted to capture these three, but Qing didn't feel up to that sort of game.

He was about to transform, about to catch his companions up in his claws. Except that was the moment when the ground beneath them broke open, dropping them down into darkness before he'd a chance to do much more than grow his horns.

As he fell, shifting as he went, Qing could only hope his Master had found a way into the Imperial City after all.

CHAPTER 13
Confrontation

It didn't surprise Zhi Wenku when her apprentice's search led straight into the Imperial City. Daoping had controlled the place entirely once. If her preparations for escape were hidden anywhere, they were hidden here. The scroll containing her *hun* soul, stored in the archives; the pieces of her *po* soul, hidden away where her enemies couldn't find them.

What did surprise her was how easily they got inside. Count Li's presence helped, but it didn't make sense that the guards would be so lackadaisical about protecting their charges. They were all younger guards, too, inexperienced and clearly on edge; as if they'd no idea what to do and had no one to tell them.

As they travelled across the Imperial City, they felt something flicker in the flow of natural *qi* ahead of them. "That's too strong," Zhi Wenku muttered. "And it wasn't here earlier."

Count Li's lips tightened. "There hasn't been a source that strong since I took down Kang Huang. I thought he used it up fighting me. He must have hidden it instead. My master is going to have so many words about how badly I handled this."

Really, Zhi Wenku didn't think the Count had done that badly. The region had stayed mostly stable despite both Kang Huang and Daoping. There was only so much a person could do, especially if they had to keep their own powers from wreaking havoc on the landscape.

Knowing the man wasn't likely to agree with her, Zhi Wenku focused her attention on Qing and working out what was going on around them. The further they went, the fewer and fewer guards there seemed to be. "This is wrong," she grumbled as they reached a wide open and almost completely unguarded gate. One terribly young child in a uniform that barely fit, along with five or six older and scared looking boys, didn't count at all. "Why is she here?"

The lead guard blinked. Stared wide-eyed as Qing. Tried to look menacing and strong. "Who goes there?" It might have been believable if it'd cracked. Instead, high-pitched and soft, the voice sounded too childish to be believed.

[[Kang Qiyun's right. She is a baby,]] Zhi Wenku told Shen Wei with her fan, making him snigger up his sleeve. "Empress Ling Fei, what in the name of all the Gods are you doing?"

The girl blinked. Almost tried to continue the pretense. Then, sagging a little, she said, "Keeping everyone out of the burial grounds. Except you, of course."

"That's good," Count Li said sharply. "Because I don't need to deal with you and your husband's nonsense along with everything else. Where is he and where is Eunuch Kang? Surely they didn't abandon you to take care of things."

Empress Ling Fei flushed. "Someone poisoned Commander Fan and the older guards. Ah-Zi is hunting puppets in the Imperial Palace. And that idiot husband of mine is getting chased all around the place. I'm not sure where he is now."

The mention of puppets got Zhi Wenku's attention. "How many?"

"Dozens! Ah-Zi told me to wait in my courtyard but how can I possibly wait when I don't know who's doing what or where or why or...."

"Don't hand me a clump of sawdust and tell me it's a dumpling," Pang Hua grumbled. "I'll keep watch on her."

Count Li didn't bother agreeing, just turned to Zhi Wenku. "I've a feeling I know one of the things that fake Kang Qiyun took from the Medical Hall."

"Poison."

"Mm. Yes." Count Li glanced around, clearly torn over what to do next. "We could go help deal with the puppets, but...."

"But dealing with Daoping is more important." It was obvious the artificer had incapacitated the older and wiser members of the court to make things easier for herself. "Those puppets are dangerous but we can't give her time to dig in further."

"Agreed." Count Li frowned at the sky. "Where's that boy of yours?"

No surprise her apprentice had disappeared in the few minutes of distraction. He wasn't supposed to land or do anything but if he'd spotted those puppets going after someone, he would've had to help. Nor would Zhi Wenku have wanted him to do anything else.

She checked the boy's location and pointed. "That way and down. Down fairly far, based on the angle of my needle." The device tied to Qing's *qi* was pointing directly at him and right that moment it seemed he'd dropped a good distance. "How deep is the Imperial Tomb?"

"Just one level, supposedly." Count Li set to walking, striding along ahead of them as fast as he possibly could. "I searched for her workshop after she died, but I wasn't allowed inside the Imperial Tombs. Now I'm wishing I'd insisted. Whatever that natural *qi* is down there, I'm betting she made good use of it."

They hurried thorough the streets of the burial grounds, spotting signs of a fight as they went. Whomever it was had done a respectable job of dealing with those puppets. There were scattered remains—wood, leather, ivy and squash—all over the place. No blood, though, human or dragonling; a thing to be grateful for.

What didn't make her feel any better was arriving at the Imperial Mausoleum and finding the courtyard caved in, a dark hole deep in the ground in front of them. "I did say he'd gone down," Zhi Wenku muttered while Xinglu sniffed around the edges, looking like every hackle would be raised if he were in his hound form.

"You did," Shen Wei agreed. "And it looks like we have no choice but to follow."

弟子

"A DRAGON?"

Qing snaked around his three companions, using his greater size to protect them. Automatically he felt for his link with his master, sensing just how distant she was and guessing at how long she'd take to arrive. So much depended on how much of a fight she'd have getting through the Imperial City.

For now he had to depend on himself. Qing scanned the torchlit room, finding the speaker sitting atop a dais. A scroll, the scroll Qing had found earlier, floated behind the figure, glowing softly with the light of its ink.

The speaker was dressed in an outfit similar to the one the Emperor had worn, including the mask. If the voice sounded like a man's, if he didn't know better, or at least think better, Qing might have thought them the Emperor himself.

Kang Qiyun choked as he peered over Qing's back crest. "Hey!" he complained. "That's not right."

Captain Li hushed him while Qing shifted position to look directly at the person on their throne. "Artificer and former Empress Daoping, I presume?"

The scroll turned in place, even as the seated figure gazed at him, eyes glowing behind the mask. "What's a dragon doing here? Have you come to confirm my return?"

Someone laughed mockingly, and a glance showed Master Zhan and Pan Wei's puppet, both locked up in cages set into the wall. "That child's no messenger of Heaven, brat. You've been so busy trying to restore yourself you haven't been paying any attention at all."

A small figure rushed out from behind the robed one and launched itself—herself—at Qing. The same little girl who'd carried that fan the night before, her face distorted with rage. "YOU ROTTEN BEAST! YOU RUINED ALL MY BEAUTIFUL FIRES!"

Peering down, Qing noted that the tattered robes she wore were covered with familiar symbols. "Daoping's copy of the Pot of Ten Thousand Crows?" he asked curiously, undisturbed by her flailing fists. As far as he could tell, she didn't have the power to harm him anymore. "Your fires did untold damage. Stopping them was my duty."

"Yeah!" Kang Qiyun snapped, trying to pull himself over Qing's body so he could yell back. "Do you have any idea how many of my people you killed?"

Someone, probably Li Aiqing, dragged Kang Qiyun back down and muffled his voice. Qing ignored them, turning his attention to Master Zhan and Pan Wei's puppet. "Are you two all right?"

"Oh, we're just fine, aside from being a little cramped and absolutely furious with that rotten little brat who thinks she's an Empress over there."

Daoping, or whatever part of Daoping the costumed figure was, rose to her feet and pointed furiously at Master Zhan. "Shut up, you!"

"What's the matter, little sister? Can't deal with the truth? You aren't Empress anymore. You never had any right to be Empress. And. You. Are. A. Rotten. Brat!"

As the pair quarreled, Qing reflected that some cultivators might get older but they didn't grow up. Not that he'd argue the point right now because he needed to check their surroundings and work out just what he could do to get them out of there.

Puppets sat on the ground around them; silent, still. Qing didn't want to bet how long that would last, though. They'd surely rouse to their master's call when the time came. Looking past, he realized the chamber walls were covered in shelves full of leather and wood and lanterns and potted plants. All Daoping's preferred materials. The lanterns weren't lit, but they wouldn't have lasted if they had been.

There were jars stacked on one side of the room, most sealed with wax and covered in dust. One stood open near what was obviously a work area, where someone had been building yet another puppet. By the smell it held lantern oil, fuel for the fire Daoping used for her artifacts.

There was also the faintest scent of rot and blood, which drew Qing's attention to the thing tossed in the bin next to the work area. A rotting human arm. Remembering the Emperor's injury, Qing was sure who it belonged to.

He spoke over his shoulder to Kang Qiyun. "What did the thing that tore your arm off look like?"

The young man thought about it. "Oh. Nasty. Face like rotten leather. Completely naked, too, though it didn't have anything to hide, so I guess that didn't matter. I still don't know how it got in my study. It only got me because I didn't see it coming. Captain Li and Ah-Qing would have gotten it if they weren't busy helping me."

No surprise that it didn't occur to Kang Qiyun that he'd pretty much admitted he was the Emperor. Or maybe he knew and didn't care? It'd be like him. Qing set that thought aside as unimportant, focusing on the main situation. "I think that thing was the Puppet Master that scroll mentioned. I think that thing over there is the Puppet Master. I think Daoping's scroll is using it to talk to us."

"I think you're right," Captain Li muttered back. "What do we do about it?"

"First off? Find out what Daoping wants. What do you want, Master Daoping?" Qing asked the last more loudly, interrupting the continuing argument between Pan Wei's disciples.

"I WOULDN'T HAVE TO DO ANYTHING AGAINST YOU IF YOU HAD THE SENSE TO JUST HELP ME!"

"WHY WOULD I HELP THE WOMAN WHO MURDERED OUR MASTER?"

"HE WAS GOING TO USE HIS BRUSH TO STOP ME!"

"Actually, I wasn't. I just didn't want you getting a hold of it. Or my ink. Or my...."

"SHUT UP!"

"DON'T TELL OUR MASTER TO SHUT UP!"

"THE ONLY THING I WANT TO HEAR FROM HIM IS HOW TO KEEP MY FATHER FROM COMING BACK!"

"I didn't even know he was likely to come back. And I don't remember how because, as I keep telling you, I'm not the right part of me."

"DON'T LIE TO ME!"

Qing considered the three. Turned to look at his own companions. "Should we just wait?"

"I hate waiting."

"You always hate waiting."

"Ordinarily, I'd side with Aiqing-di, but this isn't the time to sit around. Can we get out of here?"

Agreeing with Captain Li, Qing searched for the exit and found one at hidden in the shadows. An easy escape. A too easy escape. Qing turned his attention to the ground and sighed. "Not without getting past the array. I could probably suck its power source dry, but Master strictly forbad me from doing that sort of thing."

"Oh." Sounding a bit disappointed, Kang Qiyun seemed unable to help asking, "Why?"

"Because that's how I became a dragonling long before I was supposed to," Qing told him. "It isn't healthy to cultivate too fast. Hasn't the Count taught you that yet?"

"I... er... I don't do a good job listening."

Qing yearned to tell him he might want to stick with his primary responsibilities if he weren't willing to listen, but this wasn't the time. "I think I can break the array, but it'll draw attention. There's more puppets all over the place around us."

"We can deal with those," Captain Li decided. "Are you up to it?"

Although Qing was fairly sure rescue would be coming soon, he knew his master would expect him to be doing what he could to escape on his own, in case something went wrong. He agreed, shifting his position so the three could climb onto his back, using his back ridge as cover. Then he drew his inner *qi* together and set to blasting the array trapping them, focusing his lightning on one spot and one spot only.

As the puppets rushed to fight him and his companions moved to defend, all Qing could do was keep blasting and hope he finished before he ran out of *qi*.

弟子

Sensing the energies in the cave below, Zhi Wenku worried that her apprentice would forget his promise not to absorb more spiritual stones. It was far too soon for him to be pushing his cultivation up that fast.

Count Li opened his umbrella and stepped off the edge of the hole, dropping down slowly, lightly. "Now you're just showing off," she muttered, stepping onto her whisk as Shen Wei and Xinglu stepped onto their swords.

"He always shows off. It's the most human thing about him," Shen Wei told her, grinning. They flew down after the man, circling the hole to slow their descent, until they came to a large chamber with a nearly as large fight at its center.

Unsurprisingly, Qing was trapped within an array, trying to break free with his lightning. Three men knelt on his back, each fighting off a dozen or so of those damned puppets, all flailing and striking and failing to get past. Fortunately, Qing's scales were too tough for the things, so they couldn't hurt him in the process.

Someone shouted angrily, "STOP THEM! DON'T KILL THEM! I NEED THAT MAN ALIVE!" The speaker was someone dressed like the Emperor, with Daoping's scroll behind them, spinning wildly and angrily. Daoping, or what was left of her?

Which man did she mean? Obviously not Qing, unless he'd transformed after he'd landed down here. It could be any one of the three others but instinct, plus the interesting points she'd noticed about the one, made her sure which was Daoping's target.

Count Li confirmed her suspicion. He dropped down to stand beside Kang Qiyun, blithely ignoring the shield array surrounding Qing. As he blocked more puppets, he said, "You are not supposed to be taking front in battle, young man."

"It's not like there's any back—or middle—in this fight."

"Don't argue with me."

"No, sir. Sorry, sir."

"And get down. Now."

Zhi Wenku ignored the pair, gesturing at the cages holding Zhan Ping and Pan Wei's puppet self. "Shen Wei, you and Xinglu get them free, please? I'll help Qing."

"Of course, my dear." Shen Wei hurried to the wall, fighting his way past more puppets with Xinglu close behind. The boy broke the things with little yelps of satisfaction that would have been more appropriate to his hound form.

Zhi Wenku shook her head at the boy's antics and headed to where Qing was working on his side of the array. Given time, without distractions, he probably would have broken through soon enough. It hadn't been designed to handle a young dragonling's lightning and it was cracking even as she approached.

Seeing Qing was damaging more than just the array, Zhi Wenku hurriedly set up her own wards. The last thing they needed was for him to crack the floor and drop them down to the source of the spiritual energy permeating this place.

Qing saw her as she landed and almost broke off to call her name. He controlled the urge, staying focused like she always counseled, narrowing his attack on the array to a slender beam of crackling lightning. Zhi Wenku gathered the excess energy into her wards, blocking everything except the array pattern. At last the thing gave in, cracks forming in the air surrounding Qing and his companions, then shattering into glassy pieces that disappeared before they hit the ground.

Forgetting his companions, Qing turned human and flung his arms around Zhi Wenku, a gesture she'd thought she'd cured him of years ago. But he'd been stressed and pushed and on his own and she supposed she'd give him this much of a moment. "Now, now. You did well," she murmured, patting his head.

Meanwhile, Li Aiqing complained vociferously and loudly about being dumped on the ground a few feet, while Captain Li brushed himself off and Count Li landed lightly beside Kang Qiyun. Zhi Wenku ignored them all, turning her attention on the raging figure on the dais, and the scroll behind her, no doubt supplying most of Daoping's awareness.

The Imperial robes Daoping wore were clearly too big for her. The actual Emperor's robes, then, stolen from his wardrobe at some point in time. Her face wasn't visible, but the 'child' who'd fallen to the floor when Qing changed quite likely bore a resemblance to the long dead artificer as well.

"I'LL BURN YOU ALL TO A CRISP!" the 'child' screamed, while the puppet-Daoping leapt from the dais to rush towards Kang Qiyun, screeching incoherently, the scroll spinning around behind her wildly.

Li Aiqing and Xinglu moved to deal with the child, the one blocking her path, the other catching her by the nape of the neck and holding her off the ground. If she'd been a real child Zhi Wenku would have intervened—one didn't hold children that way—but this was clearly the human form of the Pot of Ten Thousand Crows. Gods knew how that could be, but it was obviously true.

Meanwhile, Pan Wei's puppet and Zhan Ping rushed forward, the one catching hold of the Puppet Master, the other the scroll. That set Daoping screaming wildly, the scroll struggling to escape Pan Wei's grip, unable to control him because he wasn't flesh and blood.

"FATHER! I'LL RIP YOU TO SHREDS! I'LL CUT YOU TO PIECES," the puppet screeched, glaring at Kang Qiyun furiously. "YOU GIVE ME BACK MY CORE!"

Now they all, well almost all, stared at Kang Qiyun. Count Li and his nephews seemed unperturbed by the woman's accusation. Kang Qiyun, however, just blinked, mouth agape as he pointed at himself with a look of pure confusion. "Father? I'm barely twenty years old! My wife's a baby! What do you mean, FATHER?"

Count Li patted him on his head. "To be fair, you do look a bit like your ancestor, you know."

"Oh. She thinks I'm Kang Huang? Wait. I'm nothing like Kang Huang. I'm much handsomer than Kang Huang!"

The young man's reaction did nothing to stop Daoping's screaming. Nor did Zhi Wenku expect it to because she suspected the woman's mind had been badly damaged, both by her own death and by whatever it was her father had done to her. She reached into her Warehouse and pulled out a warded scroll box. "Count Li, I think—for now—we need to restrain her."

"Agreed. If you would, Pan Wei?"

Pan Wei's puppet inclined his head, expression sorrowful as he set Daoping's scroll in the box. "Be gentle with her, please. I think some of this wasn't her fault."

That was possible. It still didn't make this any less necessary. "Don't worry," Zhi Wenku promised, closing the box and sealing it. "It's like sleeping. Right now, she may need that most of all."

As the seal flared and tightened around the box, both the 'child' and the puppet sagged, their bodies lax and mostly quiet. No doubt Daoping's *po* souls still resided within them and would need to be dealt with, but with the *hun* soul contained they were no longer quite as dangerous.

Zhi Wenku turned to Count Li. "I think we're done here. Though I suggest you have that *qi* source below us sealed, unless you want however many dynasties' worth of dead rising up looking for their descendant to take care of them."

That made Kang Qiyun go pale, muttering, "Gods, I hope not. Especially not *my* father," but she ignored him, smiling at the Count and knowing he understood her point.

He smiled back, bowing. "Of course, Master Zhi. I did say I'd take your advice in this matter and that particular piece is excellent." He glanced at the others, glanced up at the hole high above them. Sighed. "Walking would take too long. I'll just have to carry you."

With that, he set an array, its pattern a perfect match for his umbrella's design, and lifted them straight up and back into the light.

弟子

When they left the Imperial Burial Grounds, they found three people waiting for them at the gate; Pang Hua, Eunuch Kang, and a familiar youngster. Empress Ling Fei took one look at the tall, skinny, man calling himself Kang Qiyun and clearly had to control an urge to stalk up to him and tell him off for whatever he'd done wrong now.

"Can I hide behind you, Lord Dragon?" Kang Qiyun muttered.

"I'm not a lord of any sort and no, Your Majesty. She's your wife and your responsibility."

That set both Captain Li and his brother chuckling. "It's just a few kicks to the shin, bro," Li Aiqing told him. "And you do mostly deserve it."

"I do not! I didn't do anything to make this mess. That was all Eunuch Zhao and Daoping!"

"You've still been calling her a baby and making her stay out of things. You know she hates that."

Noting that Empress Ling Fei was heading towards her husband and his companions, Qing tsked and told them, "I think you'd all better shut up for the moment." Ordinarily he'd mind his manners with someone who'd turned out to be the disguised Emperor of An Kingdom, but he suspected Kang Qiyun really didn't care.

"All of you be quiet and let the adults do the talking," Master Zhi ordered. "You included, Empress Ling Fei."

At the same time, clearly highly amused by the situation, Pang Hua said, "We'll have to set up a protected array for those last two parts of Daoping's *po* spirit. And now I look at the bigger 'un properly, I think she was hanging around those men of mine just a bit ago. Not long after you lost your arm, youngster?"

That made Kang Qiyun rub his left arm again, working the gloved fingers nervously. "I think so, yes. Why?"

Eunuch Kang spoke up. "That would be just after Eunuch Zhao formed an alliance with Daoping's scroll..." He paused, looking mildly disgusted. "Honestly, if anyone told me I'd be reporting a traitor was working in cahoots with a scroll just a day or so ago, I'd have laughed in their faces."

"That, my dear boy, is because you prefer to avoid cultivational 'nonsense' as you put it. Do go on," Count Li suggested.

"Yes. Of course. It was Zhao who freed that thing that attacked you, and Zhao who had the Black Boulder gang steal the Pot. Speaking of which, given how dangerous that thing is, has it been dealt with?"

"We'll make sure it can't hurt anyone again," Count Li reassured the man.

"Good." Eunuch Kang continued his explanation, "According to Eunuch Zhao, the scroll went missing a day or so ago and the tools he'd released wouldn't listen to him without it."

The scroll going missing had been Qing's doing and he was definitely not going to say anything if no one else did. Luckily, Kang Qiyun, as the one with the most right to be annoyed with him, didn't say a word. Likely because he was still—unsuccessfully—hiding from his wife behind whoever was tall enough to hide behind.

"What was left of Daoping's *hun* soul was in the scroll," Count Li told Eunuch Kang. "Without it to guide her *po* souls, they did what they wanted. Unfortunately, what they wanted was to make Pan Wei give them a new Five Colored Brush and the ink to write with it."

Master Zhi added, "From what she was saying down there, I think her father did something to her. Harmed her Golden Core, perhaps?"

"It'd be like him," Count Li agreed. "I was sent to stop him because of his methods."

"Does Daoping's claims mean Kang Huang is still out there, then?" Qing couldn't help asking.

"He could be. I never did find his body." Count Li sighed. "I built the Society in the hopes of keeping him—and those like him—from trying again, as well as to deal with mortal nonsense when it comes to cultivating."

Master Zhi coughed. "At this point our only task left is to make sure what Daoping left us can't be misused. After which I believe we all need some rest. Even cultivators have to sleep once in a rare while and we have been quite busy the last few days."

Given Qing hadn't seen so much as a pillow or sheet since their arrival in Chang'an, he had to agree with that estimation entirely.

EPILOGUE

It was several days after the whole mess with Daoping when Zhi Wenku received an invitation to meet the Count and the Emperor. Fortunately, the meeting would be held in Count Li's offices, otherwise Zhi Wenku would never have agreed. The last thing she wanted was a formal visit to an Imperial Court.

The Emperor had forgone with his usual costumery so that when Zhi Wenku arrived with Qing, it was to find the young man sitting awkwardly behind the Count's desk dressed in his Kirin Guard's robes. He looked highly embarrassed as he apologized, "This is terribly informal but Uncle says you wouldn't come otherwise."

Zhi Wenku glanced at the others in the room: Shen Wei, grinning behind his fan, images of flowers flowing across the silk as he greeted her. Xinglu, Li Aiqing and Captain Li stood towards the back, quiet for once. Count Li and Pang Hua at the window, perfect negative images of each other. And little Empress Ling Fei, sitting beside her husband with an expression that said she utterly refused to be left out. Nor should she be, even if she was only a baby. How else was she to learn?

Cupping her hands and bowing, Qing following suit, Zhi Wenku said, "What we did wasn't for the sake of the An Kingdom specifically. As Book Hunters, we are well aware of the dangers of allowing a malicious artifact loose on the world."

The Emperor smiled a bit shyly. "But you did benefit Us and Our city in the process. This Emperor can hardly justify not rewarding you in some fashion."

Knowing this would only go on a great deal longer if she didn't accept a reasonable reward, Zhi Wenku murmured, "This Master is honored."

The Emperor beckoned Li Aiqing over and handed him a scroll. A fairly new one, from the looks of it, so nothing of great import or use to Zhi Wenku's sect. As the boy brought it to her, the Emperor said, "I asked Uncle... I mean Count Li, what would be the most useful thing to give you as a reward and he suggested this. Aiqing, if you would?"

The boy unrolled the scroll and read aloud, "Being as how Master Book Hunter Zhi Wenku has been of great service to Our Kingdom and as how Our Kingdom would benefit from the skills and knowledge that the Book Hunter Sect have at hand, We, An Ranshi, Emperor of the An Kingdom, offer the Book Hunter Sect, and Master Zhi in particular, land and buildings where they might—if they wish—form an auxiliary sect in association with the Soul Protection Society."

Zhi Wenku would be a fool not to recognize the full meaning of the offer. By tying this potential auxiliary sect to the Soul Protection Society, any Book Hunters who chose to work from An Kingdom could expect the Soul Protection Society's aid and support. Moreover, although the Emperor and his descendants might hope the Book Hunters would provide knowledge and assistance, they wouldn't demand it.

Of course, the Emperor probably hoped for the Book Hunters to instruct him and his descendants. Probably hoped for the Book Hunters to assist the Soul Protection Society should any ancient power rise that the Book Hunters could thwart. Nor could he be blamed for either desire, whether or not the Book Hunters would agree.

Slowly, Zhi Wenku said, "This is a gift I can't accept...." Her words caused the young man's hopeful expression to fade, but she continued. "...without consulting our sect master, Master Feng Shenpang."

"I did tell you that, boy," Count Li murmured.

"You did. I just got worried." The Emperor's smile returned, a bit weaker than earlier but bright with hope. "This Emperor still gifts you and your sect the land, Master Zhi. If it turns out you aren't allowed to use it, you have Our permission to sell it as you wish."

"That much this Master accepts and gladly. Disciple Qing, take it for me, will you?"

Now it was Qing who turned startled eyes on her and she couldn't help flicking her fan so only he could see her words, [[You didn't think you were going to languish an apprentice forever, did you?]] Then, aloud, she added, "Well? Do you need an invitation?"

Cheeks bright with emotion, Qing bowed to her, clearly resisting the urge to hug her again, knowing she wouldn't allow it here. Instead he stepped forward, accepting the scroll from Li Aiqing with a polite bow before sliding it into his *qiankun* sleeve.

Reflecting that she'd have to get him started building his own Warehouse soon, Zhi Wenku bowed to the Emperor. "Much thanks, Your Majesty. This Master is glad to be of service and hopes she will be again in the future."

"That settled," Count Li murmured, "I've ordered a meal to celebrate. I do hope you'll agree? Especially since I understand you'll be on your way soon?"

Zhi Wenku didn't need to see all the hopeful eyes on her to know she'd be cruel to refuse. No one said a Book Hunter had to work every day of every year, nor spend all their moments cultivating. Besides, her disciple would want to celebrate his new status. There was time and plenty before she and Qing had to go back to Khaitan. No better way to spend it than with good friends.

She glanced at Shen Wei, smiling broadly at her, and added to herself; no better way to celebrate than to do so with someone far more important than just a dear friend. As the others shifted the furniture to make room for the coming feast, Zhi Wenku reached out and grasped Shen Wei's free hand, not needing to say a word or change the image on her fan to make her feelings known, nor to know his.

Because she knew the real reason Count Li had suggested building an auxiliary Book Hunters' sect in Chang'an. Not just to gain allies in his effort to keep cultivation from harming the common people, but to keep Shen Wei from wandering off to join Zhi Wenku.

Nor—she realized—did she mind at all.

THE END

AUTHOR'S NOTES

The Book Hunters series was initially inspired by the fact that before modern libraries and modern librarians, China had wandering booksellers who would cart their wares across the countryside. When you're in a cultivational world, of course, that means you can stuff huge quantities of items in small spaces and never have to worry about weight or bulk. (A thing much to be desired by readers everywhere, I suspect.)

As has been noted elsewhere, Master Zhi Wenku and her hapless apprentice—Qing—first appeared in a short story published in Cirsova magazine. That story inspired the previous Book Hunter novel and this one continues their adventures in a version of China that never was.

Being fond of Chinese Fantasy movies and books, I decided to continue using similar themes. Artifacts play a larger part in this novel, just as Mechanist contraptions played a part in the previous one. All with a large dose of magic and cultivation. Next book will hopefully have even more of the same, as well as more magical books getting their two yuan in.

In the meantime, I hope you've enjoyed this novel and the rather large and chaotic cast of characters. I certainly had fun creating them and corralling them into following a cohesive plot.

ABOUT OUR CREATORS

BARBARA DORAN—has been making up stories for as long as she can remember. From playing Ms. Marvel to her best friend's Captain Marvel to writing new stories for old characters (Hannibal King, X-Men, Green Hornet, The Saint, The Shadow and many others), to writing gaming and anime fanfiction online.

After ten years behind the keyboard as a software engineer, Barbara realized that her true love wasn't coding but making stuff up. So when she left that career in favor of dealing with two frequent interruptions of her life (namely her own personal Tiger and Dragon), she decided to use what little time they allowed her to work on writing. Her Long Suffering Husband, without whom she could never have managed such a goal, has been nothing if not supportive.

Along with reading every mystery, SF and fantasy book she could get her hands on, Barbara grew up watching Star Trek, Batman, Green Hornet, along with the usual Saturday morning cartoons. She became addicted to shows like Battle of the Planets and Doctor Who in her teens and discovered Run Run Shaw's martial arts flicks some years later. Those influences, along with a love of folklore and mythology, have become part of the world some small portion of her mind lives in. When, of course, she isn't chasing Tiger and Dragon from one school event to another.

Barbara can be contacted at <BarbaraDoran@sumergoscriptum.com>. Her website is <http://www.sumergoscriptum.com/barbaradoran/>.

INTERIOR ILLUSTRATOR -

GARY KATO – was born in Honolulu, in 1949. He graduated from the University of Hawaii with a Bachelor in Fine Arts degree. His comic book work has appeared in such varied titles as Destroyer Duck, Thunderbunny, Ms. Tree and Mr. Jigsaw. He's also illustrated children's books such as The Menehune of Naupaka Village and the currently available *Barry Baskerville Returns* and *Jamie and the Fish-Eyed Goggles*. He's also been a contributor to the Children's Television Workshop magazines, *3-2-1 Contact* and *Kid City*.

COVER ARTIST –

G.S. DAVIS—is an artist hailing from the wilds of Arvada. At the tender age of 15, he discovered that his calling was storytelling. Naturally he discovered this talent while trying to get out of trouble with his mother. As time went on, he evolved his talent and soon began writing comics. Now, many years later, he's still trying to avoid getting in trouble, though he believes that his wife is probably on to him at this point. So he tends to hide in his office, writing comics and putting them out into the world. He draws in two different styles: A cartoon style distantly reminiscent of the newspaper strips of yore, and a more serious Manga style, distantly reminiscent of Japanese comic books from that far away land.

A FISHY HERO

Qing began life as the little prince's prized golden carp living carefree in a delightfully pond on the royal estate. Then one day he ingested a magical soul stone and found himself evolving consciousness. With this came other abilities such as being able to take flight and change his shape; even into human form.

This would all have been terribly confusing and perhaps dangerous to Qing until he encountered the gifted Book Hunter Master Zhi Wanku who was instantly captivated by him. Enough so that she offered to accept him as her apprentice and teach him the proper way to continue his growth into a fully realized dragon.

From that moment on their adventures together were the stuff of legend and along their journeys they encountered all kinds of weird and bizarre people and creatures. Some of whom would become staunch allies in their battle against the sorcerer Zhu Khan and his army of puppets locked away in a mighty mountain fortress.

Author Barbara Doran weaves a beautiful and thrilling Chinese fantasy with truly memorable characters in a story rich with humor and adventure.

www.ingramcontent.com/pod-product-compliance
Lightning Source LLC
Chambersburg PA
CBHW051145260626
47170CB00005B/1968